BLACK GOLD

The Marguerite Henry Horseshoe Library

Misty of Chincoteague
King of the Wind
Sea Star, Orphan of Chincoteague
Born to Trot
Brighty of the Grand Canyon
Justin Morgan Had a Horse
Black Gold
Stormy, Misty's Foal
Mustang, Wild Spirit of the West

BLACK GOLD

By MARGUERITE HENRY
Illustrated by WESLEY DENNIS

Aladdin Paperbacks

Aladdin Paperbacks
An imprint of Simon & Schuster
Children's Publishing Division
1230 Avenue of the Americas
New York, NY 10020
Copyright © 1957
Copyright renewed 1985 by Macmillan, Inc.
First Aladdin Paperbacks edition, 1992

Printed in the United States of America

Library of Congress Cataloging-in-Publication Data
Henry, Marguerite, 1902–
    Black gold / by Marguerite Henry ; illustrated by Wesley Dennis.
        p.   cm. — (The Marguerite Henry horseshoe library)
    Summary: A heroic small-boned horse with a will to win is finally
ridden to glory by his devoted jockey.
    ISBN 0-689-80404-0
    1. Horses—Juvenile fiction. [1. Horses—Fiction. 2. Horse
racing—Fiction.] I. Dennis, Wesley, ill. II. Title.
III. Series: Henry, Marguerite, 1902–   Marguerite Henry horseshoe
library.
PZ10.3.H43B1   1992
[Fic]—dc20   91-4907

To Sam and Brad Holmes

Contents

1. A Haunt in the Wind 13
2. The Match Race 19
3. Eighty Acres' Worth 24
4. Jaydee 29
5. The Parallel Dream 34
6. Bring on the Mash! 42
7. The Claiming Race 46
8. The Home Place 55
9. Tribal Rights 62
10. To the Court of Black Toney 69
11. Boarded Out 75
12. A Foal Is Born 80
13. The Letter "B" 84
14. First Lessons 90
15. Hanley Webb Takes Over 95

16. Jaydee's Responsibility 99
17. Indian Counsel 105
18. The Halter Rope 110
19. Aiming 114
20. The Scare 120
21. The Wrong Horse 124
22. Golden Jubilee 130
23. The Magic Shoe 142
24. Critical Decision 148
25. Without a Backward Glance 153
26. Green Pastures 158
27. A Penny Postcard 163
28. The Winner Loses 166
29. In Good Faith 171

BLACK GOLD

This is the story of a courageous little horse . . .

    Of a race . . . two races . . .

    Of a man and a boy who were both reaching for the same goal. Each was wholly unaware that the other existed. Yet, miles apart and years apart, they beheld the same dream.

    And this is the way of it ——

1. A Haunt in the Wind

THE MORNING is fair and filled with the smells of spring. It is the year 1909, and the young Indian community of Chickasha, in the new state of Oklahoma, is stirring with excitement. The day of the long-postponed race has come at last—the match race between the big-striding Missouri mare, Belle Thompson, and an untried filly named U-see-it.

The time of year is May, and already the bluestem grass is nearly stirrup high. On either side of the Chisholm Trail it ripples across the broad grazing grounds on its way to meet the sky.

On this clear spring morning the wind is livelier than usual, swirling the grasses into sea-green whirlpools, now pale, now dark. Quail scuttle and bob along, making whispers in the grass. And wild turkeys fly above the fields, squawking their praise to the morning.

Today the old Chisholm Trail has suddenly come to life. The dust that had settled when the new railroad was built is boiling and billowing again. But it is a different kind of dust, not a steady-flowing cloud as in the days when steers slow-footed their way from Texas to the corn belt in Kansas. Today there are joyous spurts of dust caused by quick-stepping horses pulling buggies, spring wagons, runabouts, surreys, and even shiny hearses with dark-eyed Indian children peeking out the windows.

People from everywhere—from Comanche, from Empire City, and as far away as Red River Station—are on their way to a full day of merrymaking. They are hard-working farmers and grocers, butchers and printers and carpenters who need a holiday. Their women have vied with each other in preparing hampers of fried chicken and apple and berry pies.

The children have been up since long before dawn, grooming the horses, doing their chores in double-quick time, singing as they worked:

> "Hook up, hook up the one-hoss shay,
> And away we'll go to Chickashā!"

By midmorning the trail is alive with horses trotting, wheels rumbling, people shouting—all moving toward the neat half-mile track in Chickasha. Right here the excitement begins. A long freight train comes chuffing by, smokestack belching, bell ringing. A few daring drivers try to race the train, their horses wild with fright, snorting, rearing up on their hind legs.

The engineer, leaning out his window, toots his whistle and laughs to see the horses bolt like scalded cats.

As the trail nears the town, excitement mounts. Wagonloads of Indians come streaming in to join the procession. At the helm of each wagon sits an Indian brave, tall and solemn; behind him his squaw and children, bright-eyed. They have just left the government warehouse, where new farm implements were being parceled out—rakes and plows, discs and harrows. But *today* is the match race! Spring planting can wait!

Now the trail takes a quirly turn and the whole parade is fanning out around the race course. Horses are blown, men and children calling to each other, women sighing in relief that the trip is safely made.

In the more orderly activity near the track, two men are talking earnestly before an open shed. Within it stands the lone filly, U-see-it, still as a little wood carving. She is studying the two men with her big wide-set eyes, and they in turn are studying her.

The shorter of the men is saying, "Far as I can see, Al, the postponement hasn't done a thing for Halcomb's U-see-it. He must've thought a little more time was all his filly needed, but," he paused, "it don't appear so to me! My Belle Thompson is fit as a fiddle, and knows how to run. Sort of embarrasses me to match her against this poor little greenhorn." It is Ben Jones speaking, young Ben Jones who has a knack of getting speed out of his horses.

The other man is Al Hoots—tall, dark-eyed, dark-haired Irish Al Hoots, who looks more Indian than the Osage tribesmen with whom he lives. On the palm of his hand he is offering U-see-it a pink peppermint. He starts to pick off a few shreds of tobacco clinging to the candy, then laughs at his foolishness, remembering that horses like both. "Here, little one. My pocket has dirtied it some, but it's still tasty."

As U-see-it crunches the peppermint, Al Hoots sizes her up, thinking. So wispy she is, and little. Nothing about her to make one take notice—her coat mud-brown, like Oklahoma ditch water in spring, her tail and mane sparse. Nothing to set her apart. Nothing except maybe she's just coming into her power. Else why that knowing, eager look?

"Ben," he says, "she's plain-looking and drab as a November hillside, but her eyes seem to kind of follow me around, like she's begging me for something, and I don't mean just a peppermint!"

Clusters of people are gathering about the shed, exchanging family news, talking crops, talking horse. They make room for a handy-boy who steps forward, eases a saddle onto the filly's back, and a bit into her mouth.

Ben Jones starts off to saddle his mare, Belle Thompson, but something makes him wait. He understands men as well as horses, and he likes big, soft-spoken Al Hoots. He senses the man's impulse to run his hands over the filly, to stroke her neck, her barrel, her rump. "Hey, Al," he laughs, "you're not thinkin' of buying Halcomb's little critter, are you?"

There is no answer.

"I been wrong before," Ben goes on, "but if there's a promise here, 'tain't just around the corner."

Al Hoots shakes his head. "Maybe not now. But I've been watching her. Under that mousey coat of hers she looks Thoroughbred. And," he smiles, "to *me,* she's big for her size!"

A second time Ben Jones turns away, then thinks better of it. He can spare a moment; Belle Thompson saddles and bridles easily.

"Al," he says, "you already own a bunch of poor platers. And I've seen this one in her workouts. She's a skittery thing. Jumps in the air at the start and gets left at the barrier. Then she wakes up and sprints like a jackrabbit. But then it's too late!"

The dark eyes are laughing now. "Sure, sure. From a two-year-old what else can you expect? She sprints, yes. But my wife Rosa, in her Osage talk, would say, 'She's . . . '" he hesitates a long time before he adds, "'She's a haunt in the wind.'"

2. The Match Race

MILLARD HALCOMB, U-see-it's owner, came up to the shed as Ben Jones was leaving. "Ben," he called out, "this little filly's going to give you a run for your money. Oh, howdy, Al," he said in the same breath.

Halcomb was a prosperous, large-scale rancher. Big of person, too—shoulders broad, arms bulging with muscle, head shaggy as a lion. He went over to the filly, tested, then tightened her girth strap another notch. She looked even smaller under her saddle.

Strange, Al Hoots thought, that so big a man should own so small a horse.

"Hello, Halcomb," he said. "This is scarce the time to bother you with talk, but I'm just curious how you ever hit on the name U-see-it."

"I didn't," Halcomb replied as he checked the bit to see if it set right. "I bought 'er already named. John Riddle, who bred her dam, told me she was so tiny as a foal she couldn't even poke her nose over the half-door of her stall. You could barely see her. And so he dubbed her U-see-it."

Al Hoots chuckled. There was no more time for talk. Halcomb was giving his rider a leg up, and everyone was moving toward the track.

It is ten minutes to two. The race is set for two o'clock! For U-see-it this is not only a match race, but a first race. Firsts in anything are filled with excitement. People sounding important, making predictions, making their voices boom and buzz. Color moving—in the red and yellow blankets of the

Indians, in the bright, full skirts of the womenfolk, in the American flag waving.

Now the hometown brass band bursts into "Oh, Bury Me Not on the Lone Prairie," and the flutter of talk goes back and forth, loud and louder as the tension builds:

"U-see-it 'minds me of a Siberian goat."

"Better not let Halcomb hear that or you'll get *his* goat! Ha, ha!"

"Hey, don't you be forgetting she's Thoroughbred! And she's enough horse to attract a pretty big crowd here."

"Yeh. She'll make things plenty interesting for the big mare."

"Pooh! Belle can win in a walkover."

Buzz . . . Buzz . . . Buzz . . .

"Who are the jockeys?"

"Why, I hear Ben Jones sent clean to Fort Worth for Peewee Pryor. He don't weigh no more'n a handful of thistledown."

"And what about U-see-it?"

"Oh, Skinny Walker, from up on Mole Hill, is riding her."

With a stick in his hand the starter draws a line across the track. Now the people pack solidly around the course, impa-

tience mounting. Children in sailor hats elbow grown-ups for a better view. Boys dive between legs, sitting froglike on the ground. Mothers scolding: "You, Seth! You, Timothy! Stop runching under the fence. You're tearing yer britches!"

Buzz . . . Buzz . . . Buzz . . .

Only three men at the rail are silent. Blue-eyed Ben Jones, fingering his binoculars. Big Millard Halcomb, nervously spilling cigar ashes down his vest. And dark-eyed Al Hoots, waiting as if it were a painful thing about to happen. Why does it matter to me? he thinks. U-see-it's not mine. Why do I care? Is it because this is her first race? Or is it the promise I see?

He sighs, wondering why he bothers with horses at all. Every race hurts him deep inside. The horse left behind is always himself. Always the struggle is *his!*

Waves of applause interrupt his thoughts. And the crowd yelling: "Bring on the horses! Bring 'em on!"

Now the young bugler blows wild, triumphant notes, and in the echo, two horses with their fly-weight jockeys come prancing out on the track. Grooms run with them, leading them first the wrong way of the track, then turning them the right way. As they near the line, the grooms let go, the starter raises his pistol, his finger ready on the trigger.

The crowd waits, breathless, for the explosion.

With a *bang* it comes, sharp and loud.

U-see-it does not jump in the air. She leaps forward.

"Hey!" Ben Jones claps Al Hoots on the back. "The extra training did help her!"

The two fillies are running neck and neck; they seem harnessed together! Five seconds. Ten. Then a startled hush falls over the crowd as down out of the sky a big black buzzard swoops low, skimming over the track. Both horses shy. Then

U-see-it stretches out as if she too will fly. The buzzard is her pacemaker. Her tail waving defiance to Belle Thompson, she passes the bigger mare.

Al Hoots laughs with his eyes. *Run, run, you haunt in the wind! Run, run! Let your nostrils flutter and widen! Let your lungs pump! Let your heart pound! Let your feet fly!*

"You can do it!" he cries out loud. "Go! Go! Go! *Do* it!"

At the quarter-mile the buzzard is lost in sky, but U-see-it is still leading. The crowd is wild—Indians standing up in their wagons, brandishing their shiny tools, men and women yelling.

"They're yelling too soon," Ben shouts as Belle Thompson begins moving up.

Belle Thompson gaining, gaining, gaining, until Al Hoots cannot see the little filly at all, so closely are they lapped. Suddenly a groan escapes him as he catches sight of her tail wisping out behind. Then he sees her brown flanks, then her legs blurring. Now she becomes only Belle Thompson's shadow—lengthening, lengthening, as if the day were waning along with her strength. Now she is two lengths behind and the race is over! Belle Thompson wins.

3. Eighty Acres' Worth

AL HOOTS closed his eyes a moment in the familiar disappointment. He tried to close his ears, too. The prattle of the people jostling around him was hindsight talk.

"U-see-it didn't have a chance against big Belle."

"No, not a chance."

"Did you see how the little one held up until the quarter? Maybe she'll be no more'n a quarter horse all her life!"

"Don't know why you say that. She held up way past the quarter."

"Yes, but she's just short-legged enough and short-backed, too, so to me she spells quarter horse."

"Yuh," an old man agreed. "Good for only the quarter."

In all the babble only one person had echoed his own thought. Only one had said, "Why, she's just an untried two-year-old; no telling what she'll do when she gets her growth."

Sighing, Al Hoots walked away from the crowd. He set out for an open field to do his thinking. The tall grass wiped the yellow dust from his shoes, and quite suddenly he felt the tug of his own fields and a homesickness to talk things over with Rosa. Whether U-see-it had won or lost, she had somehow become important to him, very important. Not for his own sake alone, but for Rosa's, too. Just once in their lives he'd like to own a horse that was Thoroughbred in every way. As he scuffed along, a young rabbit played hop, skip, and jump ahead of him; then with one bound was swallowed by grass.

After a long while Al Hoots returned to the track, his stride purposeful. He found Millard Halcomb sitting on a trunk in front of the log barn. Without any hemming or hawing, Al Hoots spoke. "I'd like to make a trade, Millard."

Halcomb at the time was paying his jockey a five-dollar bill for the race. His bushy eyebrows lifted.

"A trade?" he asked.

Al Hoots gave a slow nod.

"So long, Skinny." Halcomb waved the boy out of earshot, and he moved off dejectedly, as if he hated being reduced to a child after almost winning a race.

"Now, Hoots. A trade for what?"

"For U-see-it."

Halcomb's eyes studied Al Hoots while his thoughts spun like a pinwheel. This man had a weakness. He always seemed to put his faith in a loser. He had never owned a really good horse. Couldn't seem to pick a winner. If *he* liked U-see-it, she might not be so good after all, and was today's race perhaps a forecast? Hedging for time, he pulled out his watch, looked at it, held it up to his ear; then squinting against the sun, he checked man's time against sun time. "What did you have in mind, Hoots?" he asked. "What kind of trade?"

"A piece of land. Land from the Home Place at Skiatook."

"Have you talked to Rosa?"

"No, but Rosa and me—we have a little agreement between us. Horses *and* land is the best Indian money. She would like the filly, I know. U-see-it is built fine, if little. More like an Indian pony should be."

"How many acres, Hoots?"

"Forty I think would be fair."

Halcomb smiled, then laughed aloud. "You're just making a joke." He waved his broad-fingered hand. It was the same kind of wave he had given Skinny Walker. It said, "Be off with you, Al." He tucked his watch back into his vest pocket and took a dozen steps away from the barn.

Al Hoots followed at his heels. "Fifty acres?" he asked.

The lion head with its shock of hair swiveled right and left, saying a vehement No. And the broad shoulders swung around, nearly bumping into Hoots. "Don't forget she's Thoroughbred!" he said almost angrily. "She's out of Effie M by Bonnie Joe. And Bonnie Joe goes back to Bonnie Scotland—one of the great horses of all time!"

"Sixty?"

"You know better'n that, Hoots!" Halcomb was growing

26

impatient. "I bought her from C. B. Campbell for good hard cash . . . "

"Seventy?"

The big man seemed weary of explanations. "Why, I paid a heap more to have John Riddle break and board her, and he's the best man in the business!"

This time it was Al Hoots who turned to go. "I know my Rosa," he said with finality. "She would not like me to give more than eighty, even though she would prize U-see-it. In my mind I already see Rosa when she takes the music box out onto the porch, playing it to please the big horses. She would like watching the little one come running to the gate. She would like the little brown ears better than all the others. But *I* would like U-see-it because . . . " He let the sentence dangle unfinished. The man was not listening anyway.

Halcomb's lips were pursed. He was figuring. The land at Skiatook was considered good cattle land. Eighty acres for a green two-year-old might be good business, very good business. His tone suddenly changed, "Come along," he said cordially, putting an arm about Al Hoots' shoulder. "Let's go back to the barn."

As they approached U-see-it's stall, they saw her picking out choice bits of meadow grass from her manger. She stopped with a spike of timothy between her lips like some senorita with a rose in her mouth. Her eyes gazed curiously at Al Hoots and her nose snuffed up the familiar smells of him—tobacco, spicy-sweet with molasses, and peppermints that would be tickly to the tongue. His voice, too, was pleasing; it had a nice singsong. With the timothy still in her mouth, she looked up, her eyes asking: "Didn't we meet in the saddling shed earlier today?"

"Why, yes, we did!" Al Hoots caught himself laughing, and

the little filly dropped the timothy and gave out a high, thin whinny.

"Hey, she's laughing with you, Hoots. What did you say?"

"Oh, I was just repeating my offer."

Halcomb's voice boomed. "That whinny does it! Shows she's taken to you!" he said as if he needed some excuse to change his mind. "Al, for eighty acres she's yours!" and he held out his hand to seal the bargain.

4. Jaydee

W HILE AL HOOTS was buying a little untried filly in Oklahoma, John David Mooney, an Irish lad down in New Orleans, was helping his grandma hitch up Nelly to the old buggy and drive her to the Stumptown Track. With the boy holding the lines and Grandma holding her hat, they went whipping around corners as if Nelly were an entry in the next race.

The grandmother had one free pass to the grandstand given her by a Mr. Muldoon from County Cork in Ireland, the self-same county from which she herself had come. But the boy, known as Jaydee, had to scramble up the high board fence that curved around the track, and there he perched to watch the Thoroughbreds run.

Jaydee had an odd, almost peculiar way of enjoying a race. The colors the jockeys wore seemed as exciting to him as the race itself. Perhaps if he had owned more bright toys as a child —balloons and blocks or a red wagon—he would not have been so fascinated by the bright shine of silks in the sun. But the Mooney family was big, and there were many hungry mouths to feed. The father's pay check had to go for bread and meat and fish. Not toys and trifles. What the Mooneys lacked in money, however, they made up in fun.

Especially Jaydee. He lived in a world of horses. Even before he was six, he knew that horses had knees on their forelegs and hocks on their hind. This was important to him, for he mounted the horses he knew by putting his toes on the side of a knee or above a hock, and with a quick leap, he was up! Riding bareback!

He had a whole corral full of horses to choose from—anywhere from eight to a dozen. His father, you see, was a deputy and sexton of the Fireman's Cemetery. He cut marble . . . he painted benches . . . he buried the dead. But best of all, he looked after the coach horses that pulled the hearse at a funeral. These were heavily muscled animals, glossy and elegant, with fine silky coats and docked tails. In spite of their robust build they were high-going steppers, lifting their knees and hocks to incredible heights.

Mr. Mooney liked to have Jaydee ride them. "The lad takes the vinegar out of 'em afore a funeral; makes 'em go more stately in the procession," he told the churchwarden.

The horses taught Jaydee a lot, too. In mounting, if they broke and tried to run away, he ofttimes lost his toehold. This taught him to reach up, catch the mane, and pull himself up like a monkey. The chief thing, he discovered, was to be one with the horse, to be part of him, motion for motion.

Once aboard, his fun began. He made believe he was in the circus, standing up on the stout rump, first with both feet planted solidly, then balancing precariously on one foot. None of the horses seemed to mind. They cantered smoothly around and around until they had had enough. Then they swerved under a low-hanging branch and whisked the boy off.

Undaunted, Jaydee would leap up on another of the handsome creatures. This time he was a famous jockey, flying down the stretch with no reins at all; nothing but a tiny cypress twig to guide with.

Although the coach horses seldom galloped, they showed great speed at the trot. In fact, at first Jaydee's father tied the boy's feet to a rope under the horse's belly in order to keep him on. But in no time at all Mr. Mooney saw that this embarrassed the boy and was entirely unnecessary—perhaps even dangerous.

As a special treat—if Jaydee had helped to shine the fancy harness—his father would let him ride, harness and all. Then he had lines to guide his mount, and he pretended he was the head coachman in a funeral procession. He winked at his father as he took off, sitting erect, clucking to the horse, feeling all-powerful.

In the midst of all this joy, Jaydee's father died very suddenly. The boy had to grow up overnight. Barely seven, he had to become serious-minded and manly—a wage earner. There was a cow dairy nearby that boasted a real western paint pony to round up the cows. So after Jaydee had said good-by to the beautiful coach horses, he asked the owner of the cow dairy if he couldn't be their roundup boy, helping each night and morning to drive the cows into the barns.

The owner was pleased with the idea. He had been doing this work himself and was glad of a boy to help. Of course, Jaydee had other chores, too—he raked and swept around the milking barn. And he polished with twisted wads of newspaper the chimney lamps that hung on the milk wagons.

But when he was not working, he and Grandma Mooney were off to the races. Always he drew in a great breath of happiness as he sat on the fence, and always he felt that mystic power of the colors. Pink and purple, orange and indigo—they flowed and furled around the track like a fast-moving rainbow. It was almost as if *they* brought the horses in! Some day he, Jaydee Mooney, would wear bright silks and fly his horse over the finish line.

As often as he could leave the cow dairy, he was there at Stumptown, rooting the colors on. Sometimes, with eyes closed, his mind burst ahead to the time when he would be putting on a bright jacket to match the red lining of his horse's nostrils, and away they would go to win as the horse pleased! More than once he fell forward off the fence in his excitement. Then the dream—strong, clear, always persisting—was cut short.

"Hey, you little fence-jockey!" a burly policeman would shout. "Git back up there, boy, or go buy yourself a ticket!"

5. *The Parallel Dream*

JAYDEE'S DREAM, like the dream of Al Hoots, was only in its beginning stage. Yet their dreams ran parallel to each other like the hard, shining tracks of a railroad. Perhaps, in the distance of time, they would converge, as tracks do.

While the boy worked the sun up and down at the cow dairy in New Orleans, the man watched over his farm at Skiatook and trained his small string of horses. Never before had his hopes centered so in one horse. "Don't put all your eggs in one basket," he used to say to other horsemen. Now he had all but forgotten his motto. U-see-it was his youngest, his favorite, and he found himself planning for her the way a parent plans for the child who is handicapped by littleness or plainness. He would have to get a trainer for her, a good one—a trainer who would recognize and be so excited by her possibilities that he would be willing to work the clock around—a man who would love her for her eagerness as Hoots himself did.

For a few months he decided to baby her with no work at all, so he turned her out to roll and romp with the other horses. She seemed as pleased as a child let out of school—playing all day in sun and rain, and in snow, too. There was, of course, a big roomy shelter where she could come and go as she liked. But she seldom used it! She liked weather, all kinds. With her tail to the slanting snow, she let it pile up on her back until she looked like a race horse under a white blanket.

As for her diet, there was delicious bluestem grass in summer and corn and hay in winter. And there was the clear-flowing Hominy Creek to drink from.

Life at Skiatook was good! On twilit evenings Rosa came out on the porch and cranked her music box. The tinkly notes made U-see-it and all the other horses come flying across the meadow. Once at the gate, U-see-it remained very still, her head resting on the top rail, her delicate ears pricked sharply to pull in all the melody.

Rosa's eyes laughed. "When they come galloping in," she told her husband, "the other horses, they *lumber* alongside her."

It pleased Al the way Rosa loved U-see-it. As for him, he was building the filly's whole future on the look in her eye. The eagle look will make up for littleness, he thought.

"Yes!" he told U-see-it. "You may have to take two strides to the other horses' one, but I know you can do it."

One sleepless night, as Al Hoots lay listening to the wind in the cottonwood tree, a happy idea came to him. The very man to train U-see-it was none other than old Hanley Webb. Good old bald-headed, bow-legged Hanley Webb, who had lost two fingers in a 'coon hunt. He had neither chick nor child to care for. Why, Webb had complained as recently as the last race meeting: "Al, sometimes I get mighty tired being County Sheriff and coming home to no one but me. Yuh, I get mighty tired of it. Sometimes I think I'd like to turn in my silver star and quit the constabulary for good."

"But what would you do?" Hoots had asked him.

The answer had come without hesitation. "What I'd like," he had said, "what I'd really like is to be nursemaid to a good smart horse—to walk him cool, to groom him, and to train him up until he'd be *my* handiwork to take a pride in!"

And so, in less than a month Hanley Webb arrived, bag and baggage, eager to begin. The first thing he did was to grade a track in the field behind the shed. Then he hired an old wizened Indian, named Chief Johnson, to be U-see-it's exercise boy. Now each day, rain or shine, she was put to work. First she had to run clockwise of the track, then counterclockwise, until she began to sense that running was her business in life. Even in winter there was scarcely any let-up. Hanley Webb threw straw on the frozen track to cushion it, and schooling went on just the same.

The combination of work and freedom after work and friends, both four- and two-legged, agreed with the little mare. By the time she was three years old her whole appearance had changed. The wispy look was gone! Now she had developed

36

into a well-formed mare, round and solid as an apple. And her eyes, always beautiful, became so full of health and liquid light that one was stopped by their brilliance. Even the brownness of her coat had taken on a nice shine, like a plain brown boulder made glossy by the water that flows over it.

But most remarkable of all was her spirit. She *wanted* to race! First she won on little straightaway tracks hewn out of the wilderness. Then on half-mile tracks at county fairs. Then she was entered at the big race meetings—at Tulsey Town, at Enid, at Oklahoma City. And at last she was too fast for Oklahoma! She was shipped to New Orleans and Chicago and to far-away places, like Juarez down in Mexico, and Calgary up in Canada.

With each race she earned a new nickname—Twinkle Toes, Hummingbird, Comet, Sandpiper.

On and on she went, winning from quarter horses and from Thoroughbreds. Al Hoots was in an ecstasy of pride over his

mare that looked so little and raced so big. He beamed at the gentle joshing about her. "How's the light o' your life?" he was asked. "How's the apple o' yer eye? Ain't Rosa jealous?"

There was only one racing mare that spelled defeat for her. She was Pan Zaretta, known as the Queen of Texas, and of pretty nearly everywhere else. She was big-going as the state itself, with no less than a twenty-foot stride.

Old Man Webb took a sharp dislike to her. "I wouldn't trade our Twinkle Toes," he said loyally, "for all the Pan Zarettas in Texas!"

The years of racing and travel went by. Good years for everyone at Skiatook. One night when Webb and U-see-it had gone on ahead to Juarez, Al Hoots was trying to figure up the number of times his mare had finished first. He and Rosa were sitting at the supper table, just the two of them, and he was jotting down the names of cities on the back of an old calendar. Rosa was spooning up second helpings of boiled hominy with pork, while Buster, their bob-tailed pup, looked on hopefully.

"Rosa!" Al pronounced between mouthfuls. "Think on it! As near as I can figure, U-see-it has won thirty-four races for us! That's meant enough money to mend fences and buy feed for our whole string of laggards."

Rosa stopped in the midst of stirring her coffee. She laid down her spoon quietly in the saucer. Slowly, thoughtfully, she said, "Now, Al, now would be the time to bring her back to the Home Place. Now—while she is the winner."

The house suddenly went quiet. Outside in the cottonwood tree a bluejay whistled, "G'night! G'night!" And the red puppy spoke for a piece of meat.

Al looked at Rosa beseechingly, thinking of her Indian wis-

dom. Was it a foreboding she had? "I wish somehow you hadn't said that, Rosa."

"I think not only of my love for U-see-it."

"No?"

"I think you need to come home, too, Al."

"*I* need to come home?"

She named the reasons slowly, with a pause after each. "Yes. The long grind of the circuit . . . the traveling . . .

the dust worsening your cough . . . the long hours . . . the cold food served to you warm and the hot food served cold. No squash and hominy. None of the good things the Osage eats. And"—after a long pause—"I miss you . . . both."

Al Hoots looked at his wife and nodded. Everything she had said was true. But his plans were made. U-see-it and Hanley Webb were already on their way to Juarez, and he had committed himself to go, too. It was the last race meeting of the season and he was leaving in the morning.

He could not answer her. He took a marrowbone from his plate, licked the hominy from it and made a peace offering to the pup.

The bluejay called his "G'night" again, and somewhere afar off a coyote cried.

After a long while he managed to explain. "It's the last race meeting, Rosa. I promised to enter her. I have to leave in the morning."

He went tiredly up the stairs to pack his bag. When this was done, he strapped his deer rifle to it. Next best to chicken and pork Hanley Webb liked deer steak, and there might be time for hunting.

6. Bring on the Mash!

JAYDEE, AT HOME in New Orleans, was too busy to notice a short news item in the *Times Picayune*. The story was about a race at Juarez involving a mare called U-see-it, whom he had seen once or twice.

By now Jaydee had graduated from his work at the cow dairy and was handy-boy at the big Fair Grounds racing park. He was employed by a Mr. Kelly who owned a stable of four horses. This job Jaydee considered no work at all, even though it routed him out of his warm bed before dawn.

Each day began the very same way. With a rolled newspaper full of carrots or turnips under his arm, he caught the trolley car, paid his nickel, and went bumping along Canal Street—past the Fireman's Cemetery where his father had worked, up City Park Lane, past the big oaks where the French duelists had fought for their honor. And at last the trolley went rumbling onto a little wooden bridge. Here he always pushed the bell for the motorman to stop, then hopped out on the far side of the bridge and walked into the Fair Grounds, whistling his arrival.

Snorting and pawing in expectancy, four sleek race horses awaited him. It was the nicest time of day for them, and for Jaydee, too. First, he watered them and gave them a big measure of oats. As they ate, he picked up their feet and cleaned out their hoofs. Then he brushed their coats, combed their tails, and turned them out into the grassy centerfield.

While they played, he made up their beds—fluffing up the straw, tossing out the soiled, spreading fresh straw to a comfortable depth. This done, he searched behind the barns for old fence boards and pieces of cypress and pine. These he chopped into kindling and firewood and laid a fire at a safe distance from the barn. But he did not light it.

Next, into a big iron kettle he poured whole flaxseed, adding crushed oats, corn kernels, bran, and a handful of salt. Lastly he topped the mixture with the sliced carrots or turnips he had brought from home. Since he used the whole flaxseed instead of the meal, it meant that the mash would have to bubble and brew for two or three hours to be ready.

Often, as Jaydee sprinkled in the salt or sank his fingers deep into the mash to mix it thoroughly, he thought like a horse. "Tonight'll be kind of cold, and I will come loping in for my supper. The mash will be warm and delicious, first as I slobber

43

it up, then as it warms my throat and stummick." In his
thoughts he always said "stummick." Only at school he said
"stomach." But there he was not a horse.

At school he had a friend who, for a dime, would go out
to Fair Grounds Park at four o'clock in the afternoon and light

the well-laid fire to cook the mash. Meanwhile, Jaydee went to work at his second job as a Western Union messenger. He earned two cents on each telegram, and all the time he went criss-crossing over the city a feeling of hurry, even of desperation, raced through his being. If he pedaled hard and fast, if he ran up the steps with pencil and telegram outthrust, if he raced back for more messages, he would not only earn more, but he might make the time pass more quickly.

Instead it always dragged out endlessly, until by five-thirty, when he turned in his Western Union cap and blouse, he was all thumbs. In his hurry to get out of his uniform, the string in the waist of the blouse often pulled out and he would have to bundle it up and take it home to Grandma Mooney to fix.

But once he was headed back to the Fair Grounds in the cool twilit evenings, he gave a great deep sigh of joy. The good smell of cypress smoke and bubbling mash drifted toward him as he hurried to the track, whistling loudly, "Pony Boy, Pony Boy, won't you be my Pony Boy?"

The horses knew the tune and the sound of his footsteps. "Bring on the mash! Bring it on, boy!" they bugled through their noses as they galloped to the fence rail and stomped in impatience.

And so for Jaydee the days passed in such busyness that the shocking news article about the claiming race at Juarez went unnoticed—even though he used the very same paper as a scoop in which to carry the sliced carrots to his horses.

7. The Claiming Race

THE NEWSPAPER article itself ran only two short paragraphs and covered only the afternoon of the race. But it might well have begun in the early morning of that special day.

Down at Juarez the morning was blowy. Gusts of wind whipped up spirals of dust and sent them swirling around the walls of U-see-it's stall. They made her sneeze, and it was more a filly's sneeze than a full-grown mare's.

Al Hoots smiled as he looked over the half-door. Even U-see-it's sneezes had an endearing quality for him. Then a shadow passed like a cloud across his face. He spoke his thoughts to Hanley Webb, who sat cross-legged in the straw, rubbing the mare's forelegs, putting on the clean bandages, readying her for the afternoon's race.

"Whenever Rosa and I have talked about claiming races," Al Hoots remarked, "it seemed crazy to her that a man who loves his horse would enter her in a race like that." He expected no answer and got none. He was thinking aloud, and Hanley Webb knew it.

"I didn't dare tell her that this was a claiming race. I just couldn't. She'd never understand why I'd put U-see-it in a race where any of the owners could just step up afterwards and buy her for five hundred dollars."

"I know, I know," Hanley Webb agreed as he took a safety pin out of his mouth and fastened the bandage. "It'd take a combination preacher, teacher, liberryan, and lawyer to lay it out clear."

Al Hoots nodded. "I can't explain to Rosa how it is when the racing secretary comes to you and says, 'Al, we don't have enough horses to fill one race, and I want to have a nice program for the day; so I'd like for you to enter U-see-it.' When a good fellow like him is short only one horse, you kind of feel obliged to enter."

Hanley Webb patted the bandage and got to his feet. "Sure, it's a hard thing for wimmenfolk to understand. But with my own ears I heard the secretary pleadin' with you, and I heard him say, 'Al, I know all the owners in the race and everybody's your friend; nobody's going to claim U-see-it; they all know how you feel about her.' So stop your worrying."

"Oh, I'm not really worried. I was only wondering how to make Rosa understand."

"No need to, man! You have my word that I went myself from owner to owner, and every last one agreed not to claim U-see-it."

"Thanks, Webb," Al Hoots smiled, seemingly relieved. He offered U-see-it and Hanley Webb each a peppermint, and ate one himself. " 'Tis a fine gentleman's agreement," he said. "Just like with the Indians, a man's word is good."

By afternoon the wind was blowing a gale. It whipped along the track, raising a yellow dust as high as the fence rail. Sprinkling carts went to work, but their thin spattering only seemed to encourage the wind. It boiled up clouds of dust until the sun was nearly hidden. At the barrier all of the entries in the claiming race were nervous, jigging out of position again and again.

"Soon," thought Al Hoots as he watched from the rail, "I can take The Little One back to the Home Place at Skiatook." He carried her there in his mind's eye, thinking: "Around and on her falls the snow she loves. She rolls in it and then stands up to shudder it off, making her own snowstorm."

He laughed inside, going on with his dream. "The racing has made her slim-waisted like a greyhound, but oats and the good hay from our bluestem grass will make her sleek and plump. Next year she'll be ready to run again. She could never loaf her life away, like some horses do."

He beamed now at how lively she was, straining to go, dancing sideways, wanting to challenge the wind. She couldn't wait! With two other entries she ducked under the barrier in a false start. A hundred yards down the track an outrider stopped the runaways, made them turn around and come back.

Then in one tremendous instant the flag was dropped and the horses were off!

Al Hoots' lips stretched tight for a moment as U-see-it broke last, a good half-length behind the others. But almost at once the trip-hammer power of her legs began moving her forward, inch by inch, stride by stride.

He held onto the rail, hearing the caller sound her name and position. "U-see-it in fourth place at the quarter." His grip tightened. U-see-it was a small brown mouse among the bigger horses, taking twice as many strides as they did. Now she scampered her way from fourth position to third, to second. And now the caller was shouting, "U-see-it in second place at the half." She was four lengths from the leader.

Al's heart pounded and he took off his hat as if the weight of it were more then he could bear. U-see-it was going to do it

49

again, but he wished he hadn't asked it of her, not on a day like this with the wind battering her, blowing dust in her eyes and up her nostrils and down her ears. Now he wished he had scratched her name off. But the pride in him swelled. For at the head of the stretch she was making her bid for the lead. Nothing mouselike about her now! Mane whipping like licks of flame, tail floating on the wind. The Number One horse only a length ahead. Now but a half-length. Now a neck.

She was going to do it again! The finish line just ahead. And U-see-it a gleam of brown light reaching for it, gaining sharply.

But—it's too late! The race is over!

Al Hoots wiped the dust from his lips. He glanced in agony to the heavens and in the voice of the wind he heard Rosa's voice saying, "Now is the time to bring her back to the Home Place. Now, while she is winner."

After the race Al Hoots hovered over U-see-it as if the hairline finish had been a hurt that he himself had inflicted, as if *he* had somehow been to blame for the wind and the dust.

Gently he helped Old Man Webb sponge her face with cool water. Then they washed her whole body with lukewarm water and alcohol. Finally with a long scraper they squeezed the water from her coat and placed the blanket over her for warmth. Then they both walked her slowly, around and around, with no word between them.

When at last they were satisfied that she was cooled out and eating her hay, the two men started off to get their own suppers.

"Don't go just yet, gen'lemen!" a voice mocked. And before them stood a burly stranger, blocking their path. The slanting sun caught him full in the face and lighted the eyes for what they were—glinty and small and shrewd. A hoarse voice said, "Foxy of me to wait until you got her all bathed and cooled out, wasn't it?" The grubby hands now waved a piece of paper. "This here's my receipt. I paid the steward, and now she's mine." He pointed to U-see-it, who looked from one to the other with wide inquiring eyes.

"She's *what?*" the words wrenched themselves from Al Hoots' mouth.

"A claiming race, ain't it?"

There was nothing but silence, a deep, ominous silence, broken only by U-see-it munching her hay and switching about in her stall to look over the half-door. On either side of her, sorrel heads, gray heads, heads with blazes peered out, ears pricked in curiosity.

Grooms with rub rags over their shoulders quickly gathered in a ring around the three men, their mouths gaping, their whole expression saying, "Anybody who tries to claim U-see-it must be part skunk or not very smart."

The cords on either side of Al Hoots' neck bulged big. His mouth opened but no words came. It was Hanley Webb who blurted out, "Who in tunket you think you are?"

The stranger's lips parted, showing long yellow teeth that revealed his age and his tobacco chewing. "I'm the agent for an owner in today's race."

"Wait just a minute!" shouted Hanley Webb, shaking his fist. "We had a gentleman's agreement!"

"Seems my client had a change of heart."

Al Hoots touched Webb's sleeve. "You tell that man," he bit off the words, uttering each one separately, "you tell him to wait right here. I'll be back."

With face tight drawn, he walked around the little knot of men, past the adobe barns, past the row of cottage barns to the very last one. It held Hanley Webb's bunk, and on the bunk lay Al's own traveling bag.

There was just one thing to do.

He unbuckled the straps around the bag and took the rifle out of its case. Pained but resolute, he strode back with firm step. The grooms were roiled to anger now. They gave way to make room for him as he came on. His eyes were on the stranger's and he raised the rifle. "Now!" he commanded. "You go!"

The agent's face went as white as his receipt. He almost toppled over backward.

Webb cried out, "Al! Don't, Al! You can't mean it!"

The stranger, still backing away, gulped in terror. "My mistake, Hoots. My mistake." Then he turned and fled.

Hoots smiled weakly as the grooms came, one by one, to shake his hand. "That rat!" they said. "Doing somebody else's dirty work!"

"But, Al," one shook his head doubtfully, "for your own sake I wish you hadn't of used the rifle."

"Well, it's done now, boys. It's the last time I'll ever enter my little mare in a claiming race." That was all he had to say. His shoulders sagged and he seemed suddenly tired and beaten and old. He went to put his gun away, walking slow and bent, but he had gone only a few paces when a messenger summoned him to the steward's office. He knew what the verdict would be, even before it was said.

The words came slowly, with the steward's kindly hand on his arm, but they were no less final. "Even under circumstances that we all understand, Hoots, you know that a claiming race is a selling race. I have no choice but to bar you and U-see-it from the tracks. *Forever.*" As if this were not punishment enough, the steward added, "And U-see-it's name will be struck from the Thoroughbred Registry. I'm sorry, Hoots. Sorrier than you know." And he reached for the limp hand and wrung it in sympathy.

As Al Hoots walked out of the office, he was tempted to appeal the verdict, but deep in his heart he felt that the track secretary had probably done all he could.

8. *The Home Place*

HOMEWARD BOUND! Al Hoots and Hanley Webb sitting opposite each other in the worn straw seats of the northbound Cannon Ball; U-see-it in the boxcar. She alone was content. Her lead rope was unfastened and she had the whole end of the car to herself with a bale of freshly cut hay to sample and a barrel full of water.

As the hour neared noon on the first day of the trip, the brakeman went through the cars, calling out in a loud voice, "Abilene ahead. Thirty-minute stop for dinner."

"You go," Al Hoots said to Hanley Webb. "I'm not hungry."

Men, women, and children poured out of the train, anxious to get a table, needing to stretch their legs, eager to satisfy their hunger.

Only the big sorrowful man sat with his elbow on the window sill, head cupped in his hand, eyes closed. Part of him had gone on ahead to Skiatook, wondering how to break the news to Rosa. And part of him was back in the boxcar, fretting over the wrong he had done U-see-it. He seemed unaware that after a while the car began filling up again, that Hanley Webb was standing beside him.

"Here, Al, I brung you a nice ham sandwich and a cup of hot coffee." He leaned over Al, hovering like some mother hen. "I couldn't take it out," he went on, doing his best to draw a responsive smile, "not till I paid for the cup, too. So, begorry, you better drink up."

Al Hoots turned from the window and took the cup. He raised it toward Webb. "Here's to The Little One in the box-car," he said with a heavy sigh.

He drank his coffee, and then a quiet settled down over the men. In spite of the wordlessness, the two drew strength from each other. Small, squat Hanley Webb kept wanting to comfort the big man. He wanted to say a hundred things, but said none.

Al Hoots looked out at the fast-moving landscape, and his eyes, so dark and full of hurt, finally braved Webb to speak. "You could still take U-see-it to the little bush tracks," he said, "even though she ain't what you'd call a bushwhacker."

"Oh, no!" the deep-timbered voice was full of shock.

Again silence fell over them while the train whistled and chugged across the plains of Texas. Minutes went by, and an hour. Then Al Hoots' shoulders began to straighten and the weariness seemed to fall away. Suddenly he was able to speak. "Webb!" he exclaimed. "For a long time I've had a kind of dream. Why did it take a blow like this to start me aiming for it?" And now a smile and a fresh purpose lighted his face.

On the afternoon of the second day two dusty, tired men and a fresh-looking mare turned into the lane at Skiatook. Al Hoots looked about him in amazement. Nothing was changed— the cottonwood branches still bare against the sky, the fields still brown and sodden. He felt as if he had been gone for years instead of days. As the two men led U-see-it up the lane, the place burst into activity. Horses came galloping across the field to the gate. Curious-eyed, they snorted their questions to U-see-it. A mother goose scurried and honked her goslings to safety. Buster came flying out of the house, his whole being

hurrying and whiffing to find out if here were friend or foe. And Rosa waved her red apron to them from the doorway.

Later that evening, when twilight had settled down and U-see-it was snugly bedded in her familiar stall, Al Hoots and Webb went into the house for supper. Rosa's coffee was sending out its fragrance, mingling with the spicy smell of barbecued beef. The two men scraped their chairs across the worn wood floor and sat down in silence at the big plank table.

The quiet grew deeper as if something of great portent hung in the air. Even Buster seemed to sense a strangeness. He climbed into his box and sat blinking at them all. Rosa filled each coffee cup to its brim, ladled up the beef and gravy, and set a bowl of steaming fried bread in the center of the table. Then, instead of tidying up as was her wont, she, too, sat down, waiting. The expectant look on her face made the two men uneasy. They reached for the bread, covered it over with the barbecued meat, and ate heartily, as if eating were their prime concern.

"*Now!*" Rosa said, sighing happily and folding her arms across her bosom. "At last you bring U-see-it back to the Home Place. A winner. Many years she will romp in the green meadow, and then the happy hunting ground, with her music box buried beside her. Maybe so, Al?"

The time had come. The time to make Rosa see the dream too. But first he told her of the claiming race; of the wind blowing and the dust stinging and how U-see-it was going to win, but . . .

Rosa nodded her head to save him the embarrassment of saying the words of failure. "Coming in second is no shame," she said.

"No." Al swallowed. "The shame comes after." Swiftly he

told her of the stranger who claimed U-see-it, and in the telling he did not spare himself.

With arms still folded Rosa listened and felt the finality of the words: "U-see-it and I are barred from the big tracks forever. We are outlawed!"

Her face clouded over. Her man's happiest years had been spent matching U-see-it against all comers. Now the verdict was like a blight. She felt arrows of fear coming at her. The Home Place might never hold her man. Even five hundred acres might not be enough. He was brother to the Osages! The spirit in him loved a fast horse.

Through the veil of her Indian shyness she tried to speak her thoughts. "Al," she said, "held down here at Skiatook, you will be like the old Indian who walked away from his teepee. Never was he found again. The footprints just stopped. They—just stopped. 'Sky took him,' his chief said; and the place where footprints ended was ever afterward named Skiatook."

For a long moment no one spoke. Only the little dog whimpered in his dream.

Rosa was puzzled. Why was not her man more troubled? Why was there the shine of hope in the tired eyes? Why the secret, glowing look? Why? She turned questioningly to Hanley Webb, who only shook his head as he opened and shut the lid of his tobacco can.

And then the deep, husky voice began again. "U-see-it's speed is *not* over and done with. It shall be preserved."

"Yes! In the heart and in the mind!" Rosa nodded.

"No, Rosa. In her colt."

Again the room went very still. A moth hovered over the kerosene lamp and the flutter of its wings made a whisper in the stillness.

"On the long trip home," Al Hoots explained, "I have not been idle in my mind. U-see-it shall have a foal," he announced, his voice strong and prophetic. "It will be a horse colt, not a filly. And it will win the one great race in America, the Run for the Roses at Churchill Downs." A smile played about his lips. Now he had said it all.

The wonder in Rosa kept her voice quiet, kept her heart beating calm and steady. "You mean?" she whispered in awe. "You *must* mean the Kentucky Derby!"

So this was the dream. So this was it. The moth fluttered wildly, left its wing dust on the lamp.

Hanley Webb's three fingers rapped out a tattoo on the plank table. "But, Al," he hesitated, as if he hated to smother the dream, "you can't be entering U-see-it's colt or *any* horse in the Derby! You've been barred from all tracks."

The big man looked off into the years ahead. "I know, I know," he said patiently. "But you see, the owner of the colt will be Rosa Hoots, not Al."

Rosa caught her breath.

"Sufferin' Hezekiah!" Webb persisted. "I don't mean to arguefy, Al, but U-see-it's colt can't be entered. Have you forgot her name's been struck from the Thoroughbred Registry?"

Al Hoots laughed as if nothing could destroy his dream. "When U-see-it is in foal," he said, "the men who sit in high places passing judgment on the names in the Registry—they will forgive her. Even if they can't forgive me."

Old Man Webb slapped the palm of his hand on the table. He liked that. In his day he had gone to Sunday School, and now he misquoted the Big Book in obvious enjoyment. "Verily, verily," he boomed out in deep solemnity, "the sins of the owners shall not be visited upon the fillies and foals."

Al Hoots said, "Only one thing to slow the dream a little while."

"What's that?" Rosa asked.

"Money."

"Money for what?"

"It will take a pile of money to send U-see-it all the way to Kentucky. Up there at Colonel Bradley's farm is the stallion that must sire her colt. His name is Black Toney. Somehow we'll send her there. And, Webb," he added, "we will want you to stay on with U-see-it and train her colt. We'll manage it somehow. Won't we, Rosa?"

9. Tribal Rights

DOWN IN New Orleans Jaydee had only one job now, and that was with the horses.

"Why couldn't Jaydee learn to be a postman, or a trolley car conductor, or maybe a bank messenger?" his mother asked of Grandma Mooney. "Each night, then, he could come home to some nice lamb stew with onions, and boiled potatoes, and hot soda bread with wild strawberry jam."

"The good Lord knows best," Grandma Mooney chuckled as she sat perched like a bird on the edge of her rocker. "Yes, the good Lord knows, and all the leprechauns in Ireland. How else can the Irishman in little Jaydee live on? How else, indeed!" She picked up her sewing and tried threading her needle. "Mooneys and horses," she said, "fit together snug as teaspoons."

"I just can't figure you, Granny. Putting your 'yes' to Jaydee's wanting to be a jockey."

The answering words spilled out in a rush, like a confession she had been wanting to make for a long time. "More'n likely 'tis my fault, daughter. 'Member the times him and me would hook up Nelly to the old buggy and race over to the Stumptown Track? Well, us Mooneys always was horse people, and we got it to be thankful for." She bit off a piece of thread as if she were biting off an idea. "A man or boy who likes to muck out and do for a horse has got a streak o' goodness in him so wide there ain't no room for any little mean nigglin' traits. Mooney men always give their horses a good ride. If they win, 'tis a fair win, and if they get beat, you can bet yer bottom dollar 'tis on the level."

Jaydee's mother somehow found comfort in this, and the boy was let alone.

Seven days a week he worked as a handy-boy at the Fair Grounds Park. He walked the horses cool. He rubbed their legs. He washed out their bandages. He cleaned their saddles and bridles. He watered them, fed them, bedded them down, and talked to them.

And soon he was up on their backs, riding them—first, under the sheds to get them shed broke, and at long last, out on the track, jogging them, galloping them, teaching them how to break from the barrier.

63

He lived in a world of good sounds and smells and sights. The creak of leather, the pound of hoofs, the hay-sweet smell, the golden straw smell, and the acrid barn smell; and early morning mist and the morning star and the moon still shining and boys whistling and birds singing and horses bugling.

Here with the horses was time to dream and time to prepare for his dream. In practice races he learned that the good horses timed themselves—knew when to move and how to move. And day by day Jaydee was developing a stop watch in his head. In a workout if the trainer said, "Jaydee, start slow. I don't want you to work this horse too fast," the boy obeyed exactly. Then as the trainer signaled him to pull up, Jaydee would say, "I believe we went five-eighths in two: two and two-fifths, sir."

"How do you *do* it, boy?" the trainer would ask, looking again at his watch.

"Shucks!" Jaydee would blush. "Lots of time I miss it by a second or two."

As an apprentice Jaydee was earning six dollars a week, and by careful management he gave half to his mother. By walking to the track, he saved the streetcar nickel. He took a shortcut through the cemeteries instead of around them, and through the park where he passed close to the dueling oaks, and then he loped down Mystery Street, making better time than the trolley car that went only by fits and starts.

And he walked home at night. Right there he saved another nickel a day. That meant seventy cents a week. And, too, he learned how to eat savingly. He even learned to like the Poor Boy's sandwich—the small loaf of crusty bread cut length-wise, with the stringy ham inside it. On some days, for variety, he bought a whole sackful of oysters for forty cents, prying them open with his pocketknife and letting the cool globs slither down his throat without chewing them. They were food and drink both!

So it was that he needed only three dollars a week for himself. The rest went to his mother.

"You mark my words, daughter," Grandma Mooney would say as Jaydee handed over the money. *"He'll* do all right, he will! And because of him some horse will become great. Mark my words!"

Seven hundred miles away, out in Oklahoma, Al Hoots and Hanley Webb were working, too—working hard to get enough money together for U-see-it's trip to Kentucky. They were cattlemen now, fattening big white-faced Herefords for market. But at night they pulled off their boots, leaned back in their chairs, and enjoyed horse talk. They got to know the breeding of Black Toney so well they could recite together the names of his ancestors from Peter Pan, his sire, as far back as his twelfth grandsire, the English Eclipse. Always at this point their voices blended together, laughing, almost singing the phrase for which he was noted: *Eclipse first; the rest nowhere.* Then on the tips of his fingers Al Hoots would list the qualities he looked for. "Good bone, gameness, stride, and especially stamina—that's what Black Toney will give U-see-it's colt, as soon as we can afford to send her away."

Then all at once the money came in with a rush and a gush. Neither Al Hoots nor Hanley Webb had anything whatever to do with it.

Oil was discovered on the reservation of the Osages. Almost overnight the landscape changed. What was once field and meadow, with grasses blowing and cattle grazing, became a forest of wooden derricks. The whole countryside teemed with activity. Giant trucks roared across the land, killing the grasses, churning deep ruts of mud. They brought in boilers and cable tools and generators and belts and pulleys. They brought drums and tanks. They brought engineers and laborers.

Everywhere men were at work, drilling wells, erecting more and more derricks, unloading and laying pipe.

And the oil came in a flood. It spouted and sprayed and ran down gulleys. Drums and barrels were not enough to catch it all. Reservoirs had to be dug and towers and tanks built to hold it.

As dark came on, the scene had an eerie quality. Gas

flames blazed up near the wells, lighting the weird landscape of skeleton towers. All night long the roaring, drilling, pounding, and clanking went on.

Al Hoots and Hanley Webb laughed for joy. Oil was money! Oil was gold!

But Rosa did not laugh. This thing that was happening was too big for laughter. It would affect the lives of many. It would affect her and all her people.

One morning at breakfast time she stroked the smooth plank table with the flat of her hand. At first the two men paid no attention. But slowly they realized that Rosa had something

to say. They waited quietly and respectfully and at last she spoke.

"My father, Ogeese Captaine, was tribal counselor and interpreter for the white chiefs. He brought this table on that long trail of tears from his old home in Kansas to the new Indian reservation here. It was on this table—"Rosa stood up now as if she were the father, the counselor, the interpreter, bringing together the white chiefs and the red. "On this table," she pronounced, "a treaty was signed under the elms, a treaty that said each headright Indian of the Osage Tribe shall share equally with his brothers all mineral rights to the land of the Osage Nation.

"Money," she concluded, her eyes beginning to shine, "is to make happiness. A good colt is happiness. Now, now we send U-see-it to the court of Black Toney."

10. To the Court of Black Toney

AL HOOTS did not live to carry out his dream. "Rosa," he
said one chill November night as he lay in bed, coughing,
body shaking under a mound of blankets, "if I die, you won't
ever sell U-see-it's colt, will you?"

Rosa was standing at the dresser, pouring a cup of steaming
herb tea. She felt a sudden emptiness and a fear she would not
betray. She came over to her husband, tucked the blankets more
snugly about his shoulders, then held the tea to his lips.

69

"You have my promise," she said in a voice so strong and steadfast that she barely recognized it as her own. "I will never sell her colt."

In the months until his death, the dream for U-see-it's colt stayed on in Al Hoots' mind. Then Rosa and Hanley Webb took on the duty of the dream.

When the time was right for U-see-it, Rosa wrote a letter in her best missionary-taught handwriting. And the letter read:

Feb. 10, 1920

To Colonel E. R. Bradley
Idle Hour Farm
Lexington, Kentucky
Dear Sir:

> *You remember when you and your horses were here in our West, my husband talked with you about our mare, U-see-it.*

> *So you know it was his wish to have her mated with your Black Toney. We can ship her to you next week. Mister Hoots would want her boarded in the Blue Grass country until she has her foal.*

> *The oil flows on the land of the Osage Nation. We can pay.*

Yours truly,
Rosa Hoots

On that blustering February day when U-see-it began her journey to Kentucky, Hanley Webb went right along into the boxcar with her. He was like a waddling duck beside the little mare—clumsy but full of tenderness.

As for U-see-it, she was in ecstasy. She loved to get on a train. It was her second home, and always she made a ceremony of getting reacquainted. First she tested her bedding. If it was made of wood shavings, she rolled and rolled, enjoying the gentle roughness and the clean, pungent aroma. Next she found the water barrel and plunged her muzzle deep, taking a long draught. Then she was ready to try the hay, but not until she had nuzzled the old man with her wet lips did she begin to eat.

"Sufferin' snakes!" he exclaimed. "Why do you always got to be so snuggly when you been drinking?" He hunched his

shoulders, trying to keep the cold water from trickling down his neck. "You're a good shipper, though," he chuckled, "even if'n you do slobber me some."

During the long trip to Kentucky he scarcely left her side. He sat on one end of the bale of hay, sat watching and thinking.

U-see-it gazed down at him in contentment. All the while she munched the hay, she flicked her ears, enjoying each different sound—the roar of the train as it sped over trestles, the sudden clackety-clack of rail crossings, the sharp *toot-toot* of the whistle as her train waited for the green lights.

At division points she even had a whinny of welcome for the inspectors when they poked their flashlight in the door. "I declare!" Old Man Webb would tell each. "She seems to know this trip is different. She ain't slept hardly a wink this time." Then pridefully he added, "Things 'bout to happen to us is awful important. She's to be bred, y' know."

At the journey's end, in the grayness of dawn, the unloading chute looked strange to U-see-it. Bigger than those she had used at the race courses. Yet not so busy. Here were two handsome Negro grooms in starched white-and-green jackets to help unload her.

This nettled Hanley Webb. "Mebbe you think I'm too old to handle her alone, but if'n you do, you got another think coming!"

"Oh, no, sir!" one of the grooms said quickly. "We just come to lead you the way to Idle Hour Farm. Colonel Bradley, he's expecting you, sir."

The other groom said, "Land sakes, she's a lively little bundle, ain't she? I likes 'em with spirit and spunk." He unfolded a green-and-white blanket, threw it over U-see-it's back, tied the string at her chest and under her belly, and slipped her tail through the tail loop.

Then with the two grooms at her head and Old Man Webb bringing up the rear, the little procession footed its way down the old Frankfort Pike. Morning had come and the grooms were singing lustily to the hilltops now touched with sunlight:

"Oh, it fell upon old master's ear
Like a strain of music sweet.
Weren't no music he could hear
Like the tread of race hoss feet . . .
Like the tread of race hoss feet . . .
Like the tread of race hoss feet."

Colonel Bradley himself was on hand to greet U-see-it and Hanley Webb. He was a slender man, straight-backed as a poker. What over-awed Webb was that he wore a starched batwing collar with black tie, and a black bowler hat. "I admired Al Hoots," he said quietly, "and I'm glad to have U-see-it here."

Hanley Webb could only nod. He felt out of place in the manicured beauty of the Lexington countryside and in the presence of the dignified Colonel.

But if Hanley Webb felt strange, U-see-it did not. Right away she liked everything about Idle Hour Farm—the roominess of her box stall with its bedding banked up around the sides so she could roll without bumping her shoulders, and the juiciness of the luxuriant blue grass, and the fresh, cool water of Elkhorn Creek, rich in the lime and phosphorous that her colt would need.

"She fits here like she belonged," Hanley Webb had to admit. He even made bold to say so one day to Colonel Bradley. The two men were standing at the time in front of Black Toney's paddock, admiring the sleek stallion as a groom exercised him on a lunge line. He seemed on springs, his action so bold that when he trotted his hoofs stayed in the air a split second longer than expected.

"And why shouldn't U-see-it belong here?" Colonel Bradley asked, his eyes following the grand movements of the proud stallion. "She has quality, too. Same as Black Toney."

"That's right, sir! She was out of Effie M by Bonnie Joe," Hanley Webb said loyally.

"And her grandsire was none other than the great Bowling Green," Colonel Bradley added. "It's about as good a breeding as we ever had."

"I s'pose, sir, you heard . . ."

"Heard what, Webb?"

"Why . . . sir . . . Black Toney and she were mated yesterday, sir."

The Colonel pursed his thin lips, calculating the dates. "Hmmmm. That means she should have her foal close to the first of February if all goes well, eh, Webb?"

"Yessir! The closer the better."

11. Boarded Out

MARCH. EARLY March to June. The days melting one into another. Cold, rainy, raw days. Warm, gentle days. Everywhere the swells of the earth changing color, from the steel-blue of the bluegrass blossoms to the pale green of the grass itself. Grazing was at its best.

In June U-see-it was boarded out at the neighboring Horace Davis Farm. Here from the pasture that she shared with other broodmares she could see over the white fence to Idle Hour Farm, could watch Black Toney trotting around and around in his paddock.

At first she romped and frolicked like any colt. There was a kind of glory in this new freedom. No work at all. Just eat.

75

Sleep. Roll in the sun. Kick up at the moon and stars. Challenge the other broodmares to a race.

Still light-waisted and trim, she could far outrun the heavier broodmares. Their slowness puzzled her. In every contest she was always ahead, not by a length or two but by a dozen or more. Where was the fun in that? Sometimes she would wheel about and come racing back to the slow one, her whole being asking: "Why are you so slow? Can't you run at all?"

Summer. Time of bumblebees and clover. Time of katydids chirping. Time of bluebottle flies. And now U-see-it's body changing, beginning to round out. Her interests changing, too. Racing was a pastime belonging to her younger days. Now she was satisfied just to sidle up to one of the big broodmares, and if the two stood head to tail, just so, they could switch flies for each other. And so the days flowed quietly by, and the foal grew big within her.

Hanley Webb had long since gone back to Oklahoma to help Rosa with the cattle. But the people at Horace Davis's were good to U-see-it. Horsemen came, and some wanted to buy her, but of course she was not for sale. As they studied her, they rummaged in their memories and came up with flashes out of the past.

"I saw that mare win at Juarez."

"I saw her when she won at Tia Juana."

"I saw her romp home at the Old Woodbine in Toronto."

"The only horse she couldn't beat was that big-going mare named Pan Zaretta, Queen of Texas."

The visitors came and went. And the seasons. Autumn in the bluegrass country. Days growing shorter. Wind blowing. Hoofs making crackly noises on dry leaves. Gray squirrels chattering on fence rails.

At the very time that U-see-it moved to the broodmare farm, Jaydee left New Orleans for a race meeting quite near her at Churchill Downs. Already the beginning of his dream was being fulfilled. He was a jockey now, a free-lance rider, wearing different-colored silks every day—the pink and black of Greentree Stables, the brown with gold dots of Mr. Littleleir, the half-and-half jacket of Doc Holmes, half blue, half white, with the bright red cap.

He was in his teens now—only a few inches taller, but much harder, stronger, wiser. His teachers had been many. There was H. T. Griffin, a good man with young horses.

"Patience is the trick, Jaydee," Griffin would explain. "Time is like a rubber band. It stretches some, but if you pull it to the breaking point, it snaps back and hits you in the face. Never rush a colt. Long, slow workouts are the ticket. Colts are just like youngsters, Jaydee. Rush 'em and they get so excited they're too tired to rest at night; they want to bite and kick and play until they're clean tuckered out. You try it slow and patient, my boy, and you'll get results."

Jaydee rode four races at Churchill Downs before he had a winner. And on the day he won he felt so good inside that he gave himself a holiday. Almost before he knew it, he was on a train for Lexington and there, for the first time in his life, he hired a taxicab! He spent half of his earnings visiting first one breeding farm and then another and wound up at Idle Hour Farm because he had always admired Black Toney. Any horse who could set a track record that still stood six years later was a horse to meet.

Colonel Bradley was showing other visitors around. He beckoned Jaydee into the group, saying, "As this jockey knows, we breed the best to the best and hope for the best." All the while he talked it was plain to see that he was trying hard to place Jaydee.

"Oh! Now I know," he said, thinking aloud. "You're the boy who rode Speedster this afternoon. It was a good win, Mooney. The owner was sitting in my box with me, and he tells me that when you school a horse you bring him back in better condition than when he went out."

Jaydee blushed and studied very seriously the toe of his boot. When he raised his head his eyes went past the group of people to a row of barns. "Is Black Toney's stall over there, sir?"

"Yes, son. Come along with us."

As the handful of people started off, Jaydee lagged behind. He wanted *his* look alone. But the little group swallowed him up. They wanted to show both the Colonel and this young jockey that they knew horseflesh. Their comments were good, Jaydee had to admit to himself. They ranged from head to tail and back again as Black Toney was led to the fence, his coat rippling and shining in the sun.

"Nice smooth top line," one said.

"Good depth to his girth; I favor that," another said.

"Straight-legged with good bone," a very old man pointed out.

"You bet, and he's sturdy all over!"

Yes, the comments were good.

But what Jaydee liked about Black Toney was something beneath the sinew and muscle, something within. Grandma Mooney would have called it "the power to lepp the moon."

He heard Colonel Bradley saying to the group, "Over the fence, yonder at the Horace Davis place, are some mighty fine broodmares in foal to Black Toney. Matter of fact," he added, "one of them came all the way from Oklahoma. Her name's U-see-it."

"I know about her!" Jaydee spoke up eagerly, forgetting how young he was amongst all these older horsemen. "I saw her run at Fair Grounds Park. We always called her the Indian horse. She's a sprinter."

"You're dead right!" the Colonel agreed, smiling. "She's a sprinter and Black Toney's a stayer. So we're waiting for their colt with considerable interest."

Jaydee shaded his eyes against the sunset. He watched a smallish mare amble up to a group of larger mares. "U-see-it!" he chuckled. "Now you do. And now you don't."

12. A Foal Is Born

THE SEVENTEENTH of February, 1921. A skittish day in Kentucky. Clouds chasing across the sky. Warm winds cuffing at the tree branches. The sun playing shadow-tag with every moving thing.

Common sense said it was too early for spring, but the hillsides warmed to the sun and the broodmares rolled and slept on the sheltered downslopes.

Today U-see-it felt strangely excited by the tonic in the air. She snuffed it deep into her lungs, then sneezed it out of her. She changed gaits from a lumbering walk to a gay trot, more clumsy than graceful. The wind teased and tickled her, tumbling her mane, stirring the whiskers in her ears, whipping her tail out behind her.

Time teased her. Time of spring. Time of early afternoon. Race time! She changed gaits again from a trot to a lope. She sailed slowly up and down the little hills and valleys, then pulled up snorting. Her breath came short, and suddenly there was a stab of pain in her side. She humped her back to get rid of it, and soon she felt all right again. But for a long time she remained quite still as if fearful it might return. She dozed standing a while, first one leg limp and then another. Oh, how good it felt to sleep, and to let the warm flood of wind wash over her!

As she slept, another broodmare brushed against her, and U-see-it reacted as if she were at the barrier and the horse on her right crowding her, shoving her into the rail. Fully awake now, she leaped forward, trying to gallop across the field. But

all at once the pain came on again—sharper, longer this time, and her body broke into a sweat.

Struggling on, trying her best to run, she managed to reach the far end of the pasture. She wanted to be alone. She *had* to be alone. This pain inside her—it was a living thing, a stabbing, churning thing. It came on again. And yet again. Now it quieted like a thing asleep, but only long enough for her to catch her breath. Then it jolted her whole body.

Buckling her knees, she sank down onto the earth, rolling ever so gently. She must not hurt this unknown thing that was hurting her. She rolled from side to side, then lay very quietly, seeing the movement of the clouds, seeing them tattered and torn by the wind, hearing above her own labored breathing a cardinal chirping, "Cheer! Cheer! Cheer!"

Common sense said it was too early for spring, but the cardinal and U-see-it knew better.

With a quick catch of breath, the little mare suddenly stiffened. The spasm of pain was sharp and rending. Something tremendous was happening to her. Something vital, overpowering.

Afterward, she forgot all about the pain. She raised up, sodden with sweat, but eased as of a great burden. The burden itself was a tiny, whimpering, all-black creature, and the smell of him had a oneness for her. It was her own smell. *He was hers!* In a surge of motherliness she scrubbed the little fellow with her long wiper of a tongue. Then she got to her knees, stood up, and bunted him so that he stood too, weaving and wobbling on his rubbery legs. She almost upset him, she was so eager. Finally, with great gentleness, she nosed him around so he could nurse.

A great sigh of relief escaped U-see-it as the colty whiskers and then the baby lips nuzzled close, finding the source of milk. Now she stretched out for her own comfort and to make the nursing easier for her little one.

The sun was throwing long shadows in the grass and the wind had died down when a groom came to take her in for the night.

He stopped in mid-stride, letting fall the lead rope in his hand. "Land sakes alive!" he breathed. Then he shouted to another groom, even though the boy was out of earshot. "U-see-it's foaled. Out in the meadow! All by herself!"

13. The Letter "B"

HE WAS black. All black. Fuzzy black. Except for a few flecks of white on his forehead. But these were invisible unless a whirl of wind picked up his forelock. Then you saw them, and they were in the shape of a heart.

"That little heart," Colonel Bradley observed, "I wonder if it's some kind of Indian sign."

He squinted from under his hat, studying the newborn son of Black Toney. It was the next morning. He and Mr. Davis, along with several grooms, were out in the pasture, gathered about U-see-it and her foal. For some time he walked around the colt, deliberating as if he were weighing something in his mind. Then he turned to one of the grooms.

"Couldn't expect her to have a big foal. But he's a lot of colt for his inches. A *lot* of colt!" he repeated with emphasis. "And I like that heart on his forehead. Could mean many things. Could mean triumph, and could mean tragedy, too. But we won't look too far ahead."

The Colonel himself tried a soft web halter over the foal's nose for size and laughed when the youngster did a kick turn to get back to his mother. "Knows what he wants, eh?"

With a pleased expression he moved off to his car, drove down the lane, out through the gate, and up the lane between the rows of pin oaks to his own farm. Still looking pleased, he slammed the car door shut and went over to the stall where Black Toney was busy at his hayrack.

"Good boy!" he said, marking up the chart beside the door:

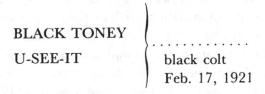

BLACK TONEY

U-SEE-IT

. . . .

black colt
Feb. 17, 1921

The stallion tossed his head and frightened away a sparrow perched impertinently on his grain box. A deep tremolo of sound fluttered out of his nostrils.

"Ho!" the Colonel chuckled. "So you're proud, too." He unbolted the stall door and watched the stallion move out into the paddock. With a sigh of satisfaction he walked up to the big house on the hill and went into the library. He unwrapped one of his big flat cigars, slowly lighted it, took a few puffs, and sat thinking at his desk. At last he pulled out a piece of stationery from the top drawer and placed it before him. With a purposeful nod of his head, he reached for his pen and wrote:

Dear Mrs. Hoots:

Your mare, U-see-it, foaled a horse colt yesterday. He is all black except for a faint marking on the forehead. The colt is but half the good news. Just today we had word from the Jockey Club of N.Y., after many letters back and forth, that the cloud over U-see-it has been lifted. They have agreed to restore her name in the Thoroughbred Registry. Now her colt can race on any track.

Your man Webb has told me that Mr. Hoots dreamed of winning the Kentucky Derby with this colt. But as you know, the shaping of his career depends on many things, including health, trainer, jockey, etc.

Naturally, for the present his mother is in command.

Now I am going to lay my cards on the table. Because the breeding of this colt is of the finest, I would like to buy him and am prepared to offer whatever sum you deem fair. Meanwhile, whether he becomes mine or remains yours, I should like to have you name him. Please send me three choices in the order of your preference. If your first choice has never before been selected, then it will be his, and his alone, in the Register.

May I suggest that if you are willing to sell, you might select a name beginning with the letter "B" as all of my horses have names beginning with "B."

Congratulations. Let me know your wishes.

Yours truly,

February 18, 1921   *E. R. Bradley*

It was late afternoon on the twentieth of February that Rosa threw a shawl over her shoulders and walked out to the mailbox. Her heart quickened as she caught sight of a letter with a Lexington postmark among the newspapers and circulars. Instinctively she wanted to run into the house to call Al Hoots. Then she smiled ruefully. Maybe he already knows, she thought.

The day was raw and puddles of last night's rain had soaked her house slippers, but she stood there at the mailbox, feeling neither the cold nor the wetness. With trembling hand she crossed herself, then opened the letter. She read it once, and again, feeling choked inside as if now she had become a grandmother, a grandmother to U-see-it's baby.

There was no one with whom to share the news. Hanley Webb had gone to town, and when he came home he brought along some of his hunting friends, all strangers to her. She could not tell them, at least not yet. Not until the right name came to her.

Locking the news within her, she went about setting the table and preparing enough supper for the hungry men. She was glad of company, even though it was not hers. It was like the old days when her husband was alive. It seemed good just to go from stove to table and to heap plates and to listen.

After supper she went out in the yard and watched Hanley Webb nail the bottom of a tin can over a bole in the cotton-wood tree. By now the moon was up, making a shining target of the tin. She stood at a little distance from the men as they practiced shooting. But her ears were deaf to the crack of the guns and the whine of bullets.

Her mind was treading slowly. The colt should have something of the name of his sire, she said to herself. The "Black" is right and good. But Black what?

She looked out across the immensity of land and sky. There were scarcely any trees, except down along Hominy Creek. All was flat land, relieved only by the oil derricks, reaching like great ladders to the sky.

Oil derricks! Her breath suddenly came light and quick. What had made it possible for U-see-it to go to Black Toney? Why, oil! Oil! The roaring black oil. The Osages called it Black Gold.

That was it! Black Gold!

Her mind was on fire now, and her tongue was tasting the words: Black Gold . . . Black Gold! Then, softly, her lips said them.

She hurried into the house, lit the kerosene lamp, and wrote them on a piece of paper, printed them big and important.

BLACK GOLD

There! It was right! Just so! Above them she wrote, *I want no other name.* And after them, *It must be.* She addressed the letter to Colonel E. R. Bradley, sealed it, and then suddenly ripped it open.

P. S. (she wrote in clear bold letters). *As to the matter of selling the colt, I thank you for your offer. But he is not for sale. Not ever. I promised my husband.*

R.M.H.

As Rosa addressed a fresh envelope, she hummed a little hymn tune, then found herself unconsciously stroking the smooth wood of the plank table. She could not remember when she had been so happy. She turned the lamp down and blew it out. For a long time she sat dreaming in the dark. Through the open window she heard the men leaving, heard hoofbeats grow faint. And in the moonlight she could see bow-legged Hanley Webb plodding down to the barn where he slept. She would tell him in the morning.

She went out on the porch and stood facing the oil derricks and the moon-drenched land. Her eyes swept the wide, distant horizon. "I know no other name," she whispered. "Black Gold it *must* be."

14. First Lessons

AS SOON as Rosa's letter arrived at Lexington, the newborn colt was no longer just the son of Black Toney or of U-see-it. He was himself—*Black Gold!* He was little. His mane stood up like a crew cut. His tail was a flat, paddly brush, not much good for anything; yet he flapped it constantly up and down while he nursed, as if it were a pump handle.

But for all his littleness, no one ever gave him a nickname. He had an air of innate dignity about him. Grooms, visitors, horse owners—everyone spoke *of* him and *to* him as Black Gold, and the tone of their voice had something in it amounting almost to respect.

Only one thing bothered the horsemen as they watched U-see-it give Black Gold his first running lessons. He ran up-headed. "A horse that travels with his head in the air may travel fast, but not far," Horace Davis remarked. And Colonel Bradley, to whom he said it, nodded against his will as if his own thought had been spoken.

But Black Gold paid no heed to man-talk. He was furiously busy, trying to keep pace with his mother. He scampered across the pasture, galloping behind her. As he struggled to keep up, the wind came at him, seeming to push him back. He blew and snorted to the wind, and he hollered to his mother to wait for him. "Wait! Wait!" he squealed. But U-see-it went right on pacing him, teaching him to trot, to canter, to gallop. Then she wheeled around the fence corners, staying as close to the rails as if she were at a track.

Onlookers held their sides, laughing. It appeared such fun for U-see-it to school her colt. And her actions spoke more plainly than any words. "Learn to use your tail!" she said,

giving a fine example. "See? Let it balance you around the curves; it's really more than a fly switch, you know!"

All these things U-see-it said, and more. "Run low, my son, with your legs and belly close to the ground. Like this! Now try it! Follow me!"

And when they were both tired, Black Gold went to her side to blow until his breathing came quiet and steady again.

One day was like another and they were all good. All frolic and food and sun and wind and starshine and sleep. Besides his mother's milk, he began to enjoy sampling from her oats bin. He liked the way he could grind the kernels with his teeth until they became mush. Then they had a good, sweet flavor.

Each season had its own routine. In summer when the blue-bottle flies were pesky beyond endurance, mother and son spent daytimes in the stall and nighttimes grazing out of doors. Being out in the dark was fun—rolling in the dewy wetness, cropping the grass close to the roots, spooking the timid shiny-eyed rabbits that came out in the moonlight.

The days and nights fell away. And the weeks. When fall came and the air grew cool and bracing, the routine was changed back again. Now as in the spring they grazed by day and slept in the stable by night. Always U-see-it was there to protect and mother her colt. Often she arched her neck over his shoulder to keep him warm, or just for nearness' sake.

But one late afternoon when the groom came to lead them to the stable, Black Gold's world suddenly shattered. Instead of letting him follow along behind U-see-it, the groom fastened a shank rope to his halter and led him into a strange stall. And there was no one else in it. No one at all. Only the big empty bed of straw.

As the door closed in on him, he became terrified. Quaking with fear he pointed his nose to the lone high window, whinnying shrilly, then plaintively. No answer came. He began running in circles, around and around his stall until he was breathless. He rushed at the door, striking it with his forefeet, flailing at it. He tried to climb over it. Whinnying, he tried again and again. Once he thought he heard his mother calling. But it was only the high wind blowing. Mouth open, seeking, seek-

ing, he flung his head forward and up, trying somehow to reach his mother's milk bag for comfort. Late into the night he still whimpered, still beat upon the door with his tiny hoofs. There was a morning grayness in the sky when he finally stopped calling her. Then in utter exhaustion he sank to his knees, fell in a little heap, and slept.

Old Hanley Webb came for Black Gold the next day. He looked long into the box stall, long and lovingly, as though he saw things that only he or Al Hoots might see—the sensitive ears, so eager and curious, the fineness of bone; but mostly something *inside*. Al, he thought, would have called it heart. He put out his hand and the colt reached over the half-door and suckled all three fingers hungrily. The old man's breath cut short as a great protective instinct welled up in him. He laughed a self-conscious laugh, then tried to hide his joy.

" 'Tain't no good to coddle him," he said gruffly to Mr. Davis. "It's got to be all business atween him and me."

He took the colt away to his new home—a fair-sized paddock behind the blacksmith shop of the old track at Lexington. There Black Gold's career began in earnest.

He never saw his mother again.

15. Hanley Webb Takes Over

OLD MAN Webb, they called him. He was squatty-built, like an apple tree, his neck thick and solid with rootlike cords spreading out toward his shoulders. He had only a fringe of hair and no teeth whatever. Of course he owned store teeth, but those he kept in his pocket.

The contrast between the finely made colt and the gnarled old man was so sharp that Webb himself was conscious of it. At first sight he had fallen in love with Black Gold, as if in the colt's beauty his own homeliness were redeemed.

With a fierce joy he began to take care of his charge. So that U-see-it would not be missed too greatly, he bought an old secondhand cot and set up his living quarters in a stall alongside Black Gold's. He even tore out two boards in the

95

partition between them so that he could look in on the colt to see that he was comfortable and happy. Rough, calloused hands, warm with understanding, kept the black coat clean, the manger full, and the bedding fresh and dry.

Each morning before he put Black Gold's halter on, he would run his hands over the young horse's body—not only his neck, barrel, and rump, but legs and tail, too. Then he would place the soft web halter over his nose and head, oftentimes attaching the lead rope to it. Whether or not he led his charge to some choice grazing spot for breakfast, he nearly always laid the rope over the colt's back for a while. "I want fer ye to get the feel of ropes and straps and hands so they'll never make ye jumpy. First things first, I allus say."

Each morning, too, he took Black Gold out on the lunge rein, exercising him in an ever-widening circle. Watching the colt trot and gallop, Hanley Webb wanted to cry and laugh both. The legs, though delicately made, were pinions of great strength and reach. But oh, the head! Must he always go upheaded?

Unconsciously the old man looked to the sky, asking the question. "Al, can he do it? Did y'ever know of a colt to run with his head up, and win over a distance?" Always he thought of Al Hoots as having gone to heaven, living somewhere up there in the clouds. So always he addressed his worries to the sky. Occasionally a cloud would shift, seeming to answer, but this time no answer came.

"I'll make it up to our little horse," he resolved. "I'll see to it he's trained so good that handicap of his won't amount to nothing."

He sent to Skiatook for his old Indian friend, Chief Johnson, still wiry as a cricket, still working with horses. When the Chief arrived, Webb said, "You can sleep right here in the stall with me—you rolled up in your Injun blanket on the floor, and me on my cot. It'll be kinda cozy that way, and cheap, too."

Next morning, when the Chief had admired Black Gold enough to suit even Hanley Webb, he explained his plan of training. "Here's what you do, Chief. Work him long hours, but not fast. We got to leg him up so's he can be a stayer, not just a sprinter. And whatever you do, don't coddle him."

The Chief obeyed to the letter. Rain or shine, he worked Black Gold. And Black Gold responded, developing rapidly into a glossy, hard-muscled, eager yearling.

"What I like about colt," Chief Johnson confided to Hanley Webb one night as the two were bedding down, "is no matter if he feel good or bad, he don't balk. If weather good or bad, he still run good."

For answer there was a satisfied chuckle.

Now once more the days were all alike, days of steady routine, of growth and development. The two old men and the horse were happy, stabled side by side. They even ate at the same time, in their own stalls, one enjoying his warm bran mash, the other two their ham hocks and cabbage cooked in the black pot over their charcoal fire.

"We all of us got to eat good if we're going to make you a champion," the old man explained to Black Gold as he looked through the gap in the partition. "Yep, we got to eat *real* good!"

So highly did Hanley Webb prize his charge that he wrote to Rosa, asking if she could spare the old Skiatook watch-dog, Buster. Then when he and the Chief needed to go to town for groceries or a haircut, Buster could stand guard.

From the moment Buster arrived, the two animals became

fast friends, playing tag together, lipping and licking each other, and sleeping back-to-back in the quiet intervals between workouts.

Buster on guard duty, however, was a very different character. If any stranger so much as raised a hand to stroke Black Gold, the small red dog became a tiger.

And so Black Gold worked and ate and played and slept, and grew.

16. *Jaydee's Responsibility*

FOR NEARLY two years Black Gold and the boy, Jaydee, had lived unaware of each other's existence. When at last they did meet, Jaydee was jogging along on an early morning workout. He felt good. It was the kind of day when he wanted to stand up in his stirrups and do pushups to the clouds.

It was January in the year 1923. As with Thoroughbreds everywhere, Black Gold had just passed the common birthday of January first. In celebration, Old Man Webb had shipped him to the Fair Grounds at New Orleans. "Sure! Sure! I know he's barely a two-year-old," he told Colonel Bradley before he left, "but *I* had to go to work when I was only a little knee-pants boy, and ain't no reason why early work won't do Black Gold a heap o' good, too. Besides, the Chief and I figger he can't begin too early to get ready for the Kentucky Derby."

On this bright and shining morning shortly after Black Gold's arrival at the Fair Grounds, Jaydee was schooling a filly named Meddling Mattie, teaching her how to break from the barrier. At the same time the old Indian was schooling Black Gold.

Together the two-year-old colt and the three-year-old filly broke away, and together they went a short breeze. Jaydee, on Mattie, won. But curiously he found himself making excuses for Black Gold. "Such a little tyke," he said to himself. "So small for a stallion, and yet he's got the makings; he's the difference between a firecracker and a rocket. If we'd gone another eighth, Mattie might've been left behind."

He thought back to the time he had visited Black Toney, and now he saw the remarkable resemblance: the compact build, the fine, strong bone, the grand way of moving.

All the rest of that day Jaydee was unnaturally silent. The jockeys taunted him. "Ho-ho! Mooney is mooning over something . . . and likely it's a horse."

"Cat got your tongue?" asked Doc Holmes, who owned Meddling Mattie.

The truth was that Jaydee could not put the small black stallion out of his thoughts. After that first morning when Black Gold and Jaydee met, their paths crossed often. By the end of the month they were in the same race. The boy was on a filly named Edna V., and although she finished second and Black Gold third, it struck him that he remembered as much about Black Gold's race as about Edna V.'s. He remembered that the colt started well but was taken far to the outside and then too late brought back in. But despite this he made a game finish, only a head behind Edna V.

Jaydee's hands itched to hold the reins on Black Gold, to sharpen him up. The speed was in him. Some day soon, if Hanley Webb did not come to him, he would have to go to the old man and beg to ride the colt. "It's too hard," he said to himself, "for me to go on like this—riding two horses in a race, wanting both of them to win." Here he was, Jaydee Mooney, a free-lance rider who could choose from among a whole lot of horses; and now all at once his thoughts narrowed down to just one.

In April, Black Gold was shipped to Lexington, and Jaydee followed the next day. On April 28, in a drenching rain and over a waterlogged course, they rode again in the same race, and again Black Gold's performance was full of heartbreak. He should have won! It was just that he wasn't ready at the start and so he had to race wide all the way. But he closed an immense gap, and if only the race had been a mile instead of three - quarters he would have won going away!

Reporters, too, saw the potential in Black Gold. They wrote punchy sentences:

. . . Edna V. scored a *lucky* victory. Black Gold finished second but seemed much the best.
. . . Black Gold came with a good rush near the end. If the distance had been the mile instead of the three-fourths, the scoreboard might have read differently.
. . . Black Gold . . . came fast in the last sixteenth, to finish second. Much the best horse.
. . . he just missed getting up front. Again . . . had to take second place.

Finally the time came when Jaydee could stand it no longer.

It was at Churchill Downs the day of the Bashford Manor Stake, the most important race for two-year-olds. In the jockeys' quarters Jaydee watched in envy and misery as Black Gold's rider put on the colors—the rose blouse with the black bars on the sleeves and the white sash—watched him go out of the building until he was lost in the crowd. Then, feeling like a spy, Jaydee pulled down the ceiling ladder and climbed through the narrow trapdoor to the roof to see the race.

As he hoisted himself up through the small square opening, he tried sitting on the edge of it, but the view wasn't good enough. He tried sitting on the slope of the roof itself, his feet in the rain gutter, but the shingles were hot with the sun. Finally he crouched on his heels, bracing himself against the slant. Peering down, he saw the whole panorama spread out before him.

Already the field of nine entries was parading to the post, Black Gold easy to recognize . . . the shimmering black coat, the upheaded way of going. Jaydee ran his eye along the

parade. The other two-year-olds were bigger, longer of stride. Excitement took hold of him. He climbed to the ridgepole and clung there like a cat. It was like the old days, the old days at Stumptown.

The field of nine is at the barrier now and the silks of the jockeys look no bigger than a string of bright beads—yellow and purple, green and brown, and the rosy red, brighter than all the others. The barrier is going up and with it the explosion of voices: "They're off!"

Out from the field Black Gold breaks well, clear, free! Then within forty yards two entries close in on him, upset him. He's down on his knees! Eight horses are galloping ahead. Jaydee clutches the ridgepole. The blood is pounding at his throat.

Black Gold is up like a rocket, trying with furious purpose to catch stride, trying to catch the others. But the gap is too

great! With three quarters to go, he has caught and passed only one horse.

Now he's stretching out, traveling low to the ground, his legs going like forked lightning. But half way home he's still second to last, still second to last at the turn.

Fast and faster he travels, moving up and up, passing King's Ransom, passing Orlox, Lester Doctor, Chilhowee, Bob Cahill. Now, in the stretch, only two horses to beat. Jaydee can't make them out; they're running in tandem. He can't hear the caller for the roar of the crowd. But he can see the black bullet streaking forward, nearing the leaders, reaching them, passing them to win! To win by two lengths! To win going away!

Jaydee let out a shrill whistle and suddenly his stomach rose and fell. He was limp, spent. He sat down weakly on the rooftop. A lump came to his throat at the great heart that could lift a horse from his knees and carry him from last to first place, to win going away.

A jockey climbing up the ladder to call Jaydee for his next race was hauled bodily up the last steps. Jaydee, eyes blazing, grasped him by the shoulders.

"Listen to this, man!" the words burst from him. "Next year Black Gold will win the Kentucky Derby. It's going to happen, I *know* it's going to happen!" To himself he promised, And I'll be riding him!

17. Indian Counsel

THE NIGHT was black and starless. The silence of the long row of stables was broken only now and then by the stomping of a horse or the muted voice of a stableboy crooning the blues.

Jaydee had eaten his supper in town and had come back, half walking, half running to the stables. This would be the time to approach Old Man Webb. Now, with everything quiet. The crowd of people gone to their homes. The grooms sleepy. The horses content.

Yes, now was the time. *Now!*

A light showed in the stall next to Black Gold's, and the figure of the old man made a grotesque shadow against the whitewashed wall. Jaydee hesitated a moment, took a deep breath. So much depended on this night. He slowed his steps, thinking. It's like my whole world is at stake. What will happen to Black Gold if I don't get a *yes* answer? Do I even want to go on being a jockey? If only I can make the old man understand how it has to be!

From Black Gold's stall came a low growl. It deepened, then rose shrilly into the night. "You!" it warned. "Whoever you are, stay away from here!"

A bald head poked out of the stall. "Who's thar?"

"It's me, Jaydee Mooney, the jockey. Can I see you, Mister Webb?"

"Buster, stop yer barkin'! The boy means no harm."

The hand with the three fingers waved to Jaydee to come on in, and motioned him to sit down on the bunk. Then the old man picked up the small leather collar he was saddle soaping and went on working. There was no smile on his face, not even a lifted eyebrow asking, "What's on your mind, boy?" There was more welcome in Chief Johnson's quiet grin as he sat on the floor drowsing and smoking his long-stemmed pipe.

The small sounds of night loomed big. Frogs making *glug-glug* noises. A mockingbird trying out a medley of songs. As his eyes became accustomed to the light, Jaydee could see between the planks into Black Gold's stall. The colt was lying asleep, his head nodding in the straw. His pose seemed more like that of a kitten than a race horse. And curled up beside him was the whiskery red dog, his eyes blinking at the unfamiliar caller.

Jaydee's fingers fumbled at the collar of his shirt. It was hard to breathe. Quite suddenly he remembered the time he had been caught under a raft and nearly drowned. This was like that. He cast about in his mind for a topic of conversation to break the silence. "That leather collar you're soaping," his voice was tight and strained, "I reckon it belongs to Buster."

"To Buster!" Webb's voice was even less friendly than before. "No, begorry. 'Tis my very own, for special occasions when I want to look duded up. Case we win the Derby, I got to look respectable. So I soaps it now and then to keep the leather soft. Why wouldn't I?" he barked.

Silence again.

"I wish I was in good standing with you, Mister Webb," Jaydee tried once more.

"Humph, 'tain't no matter. We don't mean nothing to each other."

"But from now on, we got to!"

"Oh?" The old man strung out the little word and ended it with a wry laugh.

"Mister Webb, I . . . Mister Webb, I got to ride Black Gold from now on. I've been watching him, and watching him. I know why he has such a hard time winning."

The old man slapped the collar down on the table and the rub rag beside it. The blood rose in his face. "I wouldn't let you ride Black Gold if you was the onliest jockey in the hull dang-blasted world!"

At the quick anger in the man's voice, Buster leaped through the gap in the partition and came snuffing up to Jaydee. Then he turned to the old man, his eyes asking, "This boy giving you any trouble?"

"Down, Buster. I'll handle this." He pointed a bony finger at Jaydee. "Oncet I thought you was a very fine jockey, but when I saw you of-a-purpose lose on Tulsie, you lost your chance with me."

"But I didn't lose a-purpose!"

107

"Oncet you won on him."

"Yes."

"And the next time you didn't even aim to win. You didn't even try."

"Us Mooneys," Jaydee jumped to his feet and clipped out the words, "us Mooneys *always* try. We do our best."

The old man grunted, and was silent.

"I rode Tulsie the same way in both races, but he didn't respond the same way. And you want to know why?"

Webb made no answer. He took up the rub rag, and began

working on Black Gold's bridle reins. In his corner behind Hanley Webb, the Chief winked Jaydee on.

"All right, sir! Even if you don't want to know, I'll tell you. I didn't know myself till the race was over. Then I saw why. Tulsie was calked."

"Calked!" the old man snorted again.

"Yes, sir! It was that Number Four horse that did it. Remember how nervous and jigging he was at the gate?"

No answer. Only the night chorus of the frogs, and the dog, back in the other stall, licking Black Gold's face.

"Yes, sir! That horse calked Tulsie; hurt him bad. It was a real deep cut. He just couldn't respond when I asked him. You've got to believe it. You've *got* to, sir, because that's what happened!"

Chief Johnson cupped his hands together in soundless applause. There was a stirring in the next stall as Black Gold rose to his feet and stomped.

Old Man Webb stood up to see that the colt was all right. Satisfied, he reached into his pocket and took out a plug of tobacco. With his hoof-paring knife he cut off a corner of the plug and slipped it into his cheek.

Impatiently watching this ritual, Jaydee could not help wondering if the man put one in the other cheek now, would he look more chipmunk or squirrel?

"Well, 'tain't no matter anyways," Webb said as he sat down again. "I promised Jack Howard he could ride him in the Latonia Jockey Club Stake next Saturday."

"But after that, sir? What about after that?"

"We'll see. Don't rush me, boy. The light and all our gabbin' is keeping Black Gold awake. The Chief and me has got to bed down, too. Away with you now."

18. *The Halter Rope*

WHEN JAYDEE left the stable, it was nearly midnight. He walked slowly down the road to the small rented room in Louisville where he was staying. The half-moon, a big orange slice, hung low in the sky. It reminded him of the candy he used to eat when he was little.

Walking along, he felt happy that he had been able to find out what had stood between himself and Webb, and he believed he had made some small progress toward his goal. In spite of everything, he liked the homely old man with his toothless mouth that opened and closed like a pocketbook when he talked.

Lots of folks slur him, Jaydee thought. They say he's mulish. But I like him, gruffness and all. He's a poor man's man—like my father, maybe. And *anyone* who would live in a stable to keep watch over a colt . . . well, anyone who would do that is a man to trust.

He thought enviously of Jack Howard, and after he went to bed he dreamed the jockey rode so well that Black Gold became known as a flying horse. "Pegasus the Second" he was called, because he actually flew over the heads of the other horses and always finished going away in a cloud.

Jaydee awakened, drenched in a sweat. How could one little horse take over all of his thoughts, awake *and* asleep?

The day of the Jockey Club Stake was hazy and warm with low-hanging clouds obscuring the sun and reminding Jaydee of his dream. He rode in the third race and won. In the fifth race twelve horses were entered, but to him, on the sidelines, only one horse mattered. His post position was tenth. He carried 122 pounds. His jockey was Jack Howard, wearing the bright rose silks. And his name was Black Gold!

In one minute thirty-nine and three-fifths seconds the race was over, but it seemed to Jaydee as if he had lived a whole lifetime in those few moments, as if he had been changed into an old, old man. A big-going colt by the name of Wise Counselor raced into the lead with a rush, set the pace lightning fast and won all the way. Battle Creek, Bob Tail, King Goren II, Cloister, Chilhowee, Bracadale, all ran gamely, trying to close the gap that Wise Counselor had made. But as for Black Gold, he was always in the ruck.

A boy with a streak of meanness in him might have been secretly glad that Black Gold had lost with another jockey aboard. But Jaydee was stunned. He felt like a parent whose child had a big role in a play—a head angel, perhaps, at Christmastime—and the child not only forgot his lines but stumbled and fell on the stage and never recovered himself. Deeply hurt and disappointed, Jaydee ran from the track, ran belligerently for the jockey rooms. He wanted to hit something, to punch somebody. "I've got to ride that horse before he's hurt. I've got to!" Swiftly, resolutely, he peeled off his silks, pulled on his shirt, and went out to find Old Man Webb.

Webb himself was walking Black Gold around and around in the peaceful shade under the trees. He and his horse seemed so apart from the life about them that Jaydee stopped, waiting.

A small wind played with Black Gold's forelock, revealing the heart on his forehead. The symbol gave Jaydee courage.

"Mister Webb . . ." he began.

The old man sighed. "Oh, it's you again! Your middle name oughta be Nuisance, or mebbe Nettle." But this time he tempered his gruffness with a smile.

Jaydee fell into stride alongside him. "Isn't it true, Mister Webb, that too many defeats can take the heart out of a horse? And then sometimes he won't even try any more?"

"What in tarnation you aiming to say, boy?"

"Don't you see, Mister Webb, if you want Black Gold to be a champion, I got to ride him? I understand him. I could help him."

The old man walked without changing pace—once around the cooling-out ring, and once again. His mind seemed far away and preoccupied as if he had forgotten the boy's presence, almost as if he were talking the matter over with Al Hoots.

112

Jaydee held his breath. His legs felt leaden. Just when they refused to go another step, the old man placed Black Gold's halter rope in his hands.

"If you expect to ride a champion," he said abruptly, "it's high time you learned to do for him. Now *you* walk him cool."

19. Aiming

JAYDEE HAD never known such happiness. He felt reborn. The world and everything in it was his. Sun, moon, stars—all took on a special new shine. Even the wind blew cleaner.

The race meetings at Lexington and Latonia were over, and he with Black Gold, Webb, Chief Johnson, and Buster had shipped back to New Orleans. Time was short. Only a little while until fall races. Only a few weeks to point up Black Gold's speed and timing.

Now the mornings could not come soon enough. Jaydee's mother shook her head over the early hours, but Grandma Mooney approved. "Let him go, daughter," she said as she poured hot milk into his coffee. "Morning hours have gold in them."

"Yes! *Black* Gold!" laughed Jaydee as he gulped his coffee, put his jelly sandwich in his pocket, and hurried out the door.

Often he and the colt had the whole Fair Grounds track to themselves. First they went slow and easy, around and around. Then Jaydee, crouching forward like a monkey on a stick, clucked to Black Gold, asking for speed. And the stallion, head in the air but legs and body skimming close to the ground, answered strongly.

As the sun bulged over the horizon, other horses and riders began to grow out of the morning mist. Black Gold's quick ears caught the drumming of their hoofs and the deep snorting of their breath, but he ran on, light and easy, heeding nothing but the fine hands and the warm voice of the boy on his back.

Jaydee had finally figured out his own way to ride this up-headed horse. There was no use riding in the ordinary way with reins taut. Black Gold must have his head. "Y'know," he confided to Chief Johnson, "there isn't a lazy bone in Black Gold's body, but he likes to turn on his speed when *he's* ready. I can actually feel when he centers down, ready for the burst."

The Chief nodded. "He can't fly, but he match any bird. Good, willing horse."

"Willing!" Jaydee's voice rose. "He'll run another horse head 'n head for as long as two miles, where most horses'll quit. Something about catching a look at that big rolling eye close to 'em that seems to throw 'em off stride. But not Black Gold."

One day the colt went a quarter-mile in twenty-one and four-fifths seconds. Hanley Webb, stop watch in hand, was furious. "I want endurance!" he bellowed, as he strode alongside them to the barn. "Ye're goin' to make a sprinter outa

115

him just like his mother. I want he should be a stayer!"

Jaydee stood his ground. "He's got endurance already, sir," he replied quietly. "We got to sharpen him up."

It was not disobedience in Jaydee that made him speak so. It was some inborn Irish knowing that in every race the burst of speed must come naturally at the critical moment and that a good jockey has to intensify the desire for speed. Toughness was necessary, too, but Black Gold already had that.

Jaydee compromised only a little. Instead of asking him to spurt for a full quarter-mile, he agreed, for now, to an eighth.

Several days later the old man finally yielded—not because he approved the method, but because Black Gold was thriving

under this training. Always a good eater, he now cleaned up his oats and asked for more. He slept more soundly and in the best possible way—lying down instead of up on his feet. He played and cavorted with Buster as if he were no more than a yearling. As for his legs, their tendons strengthened until they seemed indestructible.

After a particularly good workout, there was a new-won closeness between Black Gold and Jaydee.

"I'll harden myself, too," Jaydee promised as Black Gold held his head down to have it rubbed and scratched underneath the bridle. Then brown eyes studied brown eyes in a kind of kinship.

True to his promise, Jaydee took up road work to develop wind and stamina, and to keep his weight down to the absolute minimum. Some mornings he walked, jogged, and ran five and six miles and took off as much as five pounds.

"Why're you working the living daylights outa yourself?" Old Man Webb asked. "You're just a sliver! Not an extry ounce of fat on you. Besides, you know we got to add slabs of lead to the saddle anyways to make the right weight. Why ain't you satisfied with yer own live weight instead of dead?"

"Lead weight is better, I figure," Jaydee explained. "It stays put, evenly balanced on either side of the saddle, while I maybe don't."

"Well, I be a wood pussy!" the old man chuckled. "Sounds like purty fair reasoning at that."

Often, as Jaydee dressed to go on the road, he wished he were a horse instead of himself. Then he would not need to put on layer after layer of clothes—the heavy woolen suit of underwear, the sweat shirt, the rubber suit, the fleece-lined jacket, the big Turkish towel wound around his neck.

Neighbor children came out of their houses, gaping at his bundled-up look, wondering at the corncob in each hand, then tried briefly to keep pace with him. Every day on the road it was the same. Work, Jaydee, work. Bring your fists alongside your body. Now swing them up. Grip your corncobs, start slow and easy. Walk bold. Walk brisk. Heel, toe, heel, toe. Rock along. Keep walking. Now trot. Bring your knees up. High. Higher. Now run! Bend at a ninety-degree angle. Suck in the air. Run! Run! Run until the sweat trickles down your legs and into your shoes! Go another mile, and still you're not through. Go another mile, and still another.

Run bursting into the house at last. Play "Alexander's Ragtime Band" on the phonograph. Stamp, stamp, stamp to the drumbeat until your body cries out "Stop!" Then sit down in a closed room. Relax. Sweat. And sweat. And sweat!

Little by little, the boy and his horse grew lean and thin-waisted, their muscles hard, their wind strong. As other owners and trainers observed the two, so serious in their workouts, they came to Jaydee when he was out of earshot of Old Man Webb. "How about riding for me?" each one would ask. "I'll speak to Hanley Webb if you like."

But Jaydee only shook his head. He couldn't take any chances. If he rode for them, he might just accidentally break some rule and get set down, suspended for a month or two. Then what would happen to Black Gold and the Derby? Who then would take Black Gold forward in his campaign? "Not Matt Garner or Johnny Loftus," he told himself. "Not even the great Earl Sande with that cool, low seat of his, that way of hunching right down on his stomach. How would they know that Black Gold likes to take his time? How would they know exactly when he centers down ready for the burst of speed?"

Always his answer was the same. "No, thank you, sir." Jaydee's mind was made up. He could not divide his loyalties. If the black stallion was to win on Derby Day, he, Jaydee, must be his jockey.

20. The Scare

FOR THE old man and the boy the succession of race meetings leading up to the Kentucky Derby steadily gained in excitement. The sharp, staccato drumbeat of Black Gold's hoofs worked up to a crescendo. Together the colt, the boy, and the trainer could not lose.

Reporters swarmed about them before and after every race. They liked the combination not only because they won, but because they made news—the sleek black son of an outlawed Indian mare, the trainer who lived in a stall, the Irish jockey who refused to ride any other horse. Even Buster made the papers, pictured frequently muzzle-to-muzzle with Black Gold as if they were exchanging deep and wonderful vows of friendship.

The newspaper stories were curiously alike; one theme rang through them all.

OCTOBER 25, AT LATONIA
Black Gold, handicapped twelve pounds more than every other entry, *outclassed them all*. Won in a canter.

NOVEMBER 13, CHURCHILL DOWNS
Black Gold, heavily handicapped, won easily. Ran as if he *outclassed the others,* made the pace so fast that Jockey Mooney held him under mild restraint all the way.

MARCH 6, JEFFERSON PARK, NEW ORLEANS
Black Gold the winner. Carrying by far the most weight, he *outclassed the others*. Started good and slow, then came with a rush into the lead and was hard held afterward, winning as his jockey pleased.

SAINT PATRICK'S DAY, 1924, LOUISIANA DERBY AT JEFFERSON PARK.
Irish lad J. D. Mooney rode Black Gold to an easy win In a field of eleven horses the black stallion *outclassed them all,* carrying top weight. Showed high speed, rushed into a long lead and was held under restraint for the entire race. With his jockey's white pants gleaming, he won in almost a parade canter.

Never, so long as he lived, would Jaydee forget the mud on that particular Saint Patrick's Day. The rain slanted down without letup, and the track became a sea of sludge. The other jockeys took good care to wear their mud pants, but Jaydee said to the Chief, "I'll wear my whites. We're Number Thirteen, way on the outside. We'll just stay on the outside and go right on up front. There'll be no mud on me!"

And there wasn't.

Then at Churchill Downs, just four days before the fiftieth

running of the Kentucky Derby, the account of Black Gold's race held an ominous note. "Black Gold," it said, "appeared slightly sore in today's Derby Trial, but was saved under restraint for the first three-quarters, then with a burst of speed at the critical moment rushed into the lead, to win."

"He's just a bit gimpy," Hanley Webb observed as together he and Jaydee cooled him out after the race.

"It's his left front," Jaydee said, wincing as if the hurt were his.

"Likely it's no more 'n a stone bruise."

"Oughtn't we call in a vet?"

"No. No need of that. I got my own way of doctoring. *Work* is the cure, Jaydee. Lay up a man or beast and he gets stiff as a board; it's work keeps us limber and sound."

"I'm not so sure this time, Mister Webb."

"You quit stewin' and frettin', boy. We'll just work the soreness out of him. He'll be sound as a dollar on Derby Day. Mark my words. Now you breeze him only two miles tomorrow, and the next day, and the next. By Saturday he'll be fit as a fiddle."

In spite of the old man's confidence, worry settled down on Jaydee like a cloud. It even brought on a wave of homesickness. That night, tired as he was, he found himself writing to Grandma Mooney. It was a long letter for Jaydee, and heavy with distress.

Dear Gran:

Hope you are well. We were till today. Up to now I was sure we'd win the Kentucky Derby. But now I don't know. Black Gold is sore. It's his left front.

We just won the Derby Trial and that's when he pulled up lame. But who cares about that race? It's

*nothing compared to the Kentucky Derby. That's the
top. I don't have to tell you. You know it carries more
real high honor than all the other races put together.*

*Mrs. Hoots is coming clear from Oklahoma to watch
B. G. win. And Old Man Webb says all the Indians in
the Osage Nation are backing him. They almost went
on the warpath when U-see-it was outlawed from the
tracks. Now they expect to see a wrong get righted.
Mister Hoots planned it all before he died. And a whole
year ago I planned it too after I saw him get bumped to
his knees in a race and then get up to win.*

Maybe it would help if you and Mom said a prayer.

Love,
J.D.

Writing the letter helped to calm Jaydee. Now he could
go on with Hanley Webb's program, feeling almost confident
again. And so, on the three days that remained before the
Derby, Jaydee breezed the colt, let him step the wrong way
of the track, then eased him, then the right way, and eased
him again. Always going out to the track he seemed to favor
the sore foot; then during the workout he ran straight and true.

Inwardly Jaydee was glad to admit that the old man must
have known what he was talking about, for on the day before
the Derby if Black Gold favored his left foreleg at all, surely
it was from habit, not from hurt.

21. The Wrong Horse

FRIDAY, MAY 16, 1924. The day before The Day.
Never was Louisville, Kentucky, so crowded. Already
the city had the busyness of an anthill—people coming, going,
seeking, gathering, dispersing, wandering—all activities finally
centering at the track.

By three o'clock in the afternoon myriads of visitors were
closing in on the barns, studying the entries, while dogs barked,
banty roosters and hens squawked underfoot, and an occasional
goat went ba-a-a-ing and stomping at the fuss.

In the midst of all the confusion walked quiet Rosa Hoots,
wearing her long-sleeved Sunday dress, a hat to shade her
eyes, and a bright scarf made of loops of gay silk. She had

already sought directions from an official, and now moved purposefully toward the third row of barns, end stall.

Hanley Webb was holding a bucket of water to Black Gold's lips, but when his eyes caught sight of Rosa, he set the bucket down shamefacedly and came out of the stable. "Hello, Rosa! You would catch me acting like an old nursemaid," he chortled.

Rosa grasped his hand warmly, without a word. Then she stood at his side, stood silently before the colt she had never seen. The late afternoon sun was slanting into his stall, giving an extra polish to his coat. With his tail toward her, he was busy pulling bits of hay from his manger. It pleased Rosa to see that his smooth rump had the gleam of black satin. He turned about and came to the door, his friendly eyes curious, asking, "And who are you? What are you doing here?"

She saw that he was more delicately made, more beautiful and fiery spirited than his mother. But his forelock, like hers, was unruly, and there was an engaging quality in the way he looked out of his wide-set brown eyes until U-see-it almost spoke again through him.

Her hands reached out shyly, wanting to touch his neck. He did not draw away, but let the strong, gentle fingers stroke him, let them lift up his forelock and softly trace the heart-shaped marking.

Still looking, looking, memorizing every curve and line of him, she stood motionless. It was Hanley Webb who broke in. "He's just like you painted a picture! Ain't he? Not ribby and drawed in at the waist. Just all pretty and slick, and his veins a-sticking out."

"When I get back to Skiatook," Rosa said more to the colt than to Webb, "I will tell U-see-it how fine a son she has."

"How is U-see-it?" Webb broke in.

"She is getting a little old and I think maybe her hearing fails. Unless the wind blows just right, she doesn't hear the music box any more."

Now Rosa was talking solely to Black Gold. "But I will go close to her ear and tell her she can be proud."

Rosa seemed close to tears and the Old Man glanced helplessly up at the sky. "Your Al, too . . . he would feel big-chested and proud could he see her colt now. Yes, Rosa?"

And Rosa nodded.

Saturday, May 17, 1924. The Morning of The Day.

Jaydee, up before dawn, out on the track, breezing Black Gold an easy mile to limber muscles already limbered, to sample the wind, to be ready.

As he listened to the even rhythm of Black Gold's feet and felt the flowing movement of his body, he found himself shouting: "No limp! You're going sound! Sound! Sound!"

Early morning visitors were already clustered along the rail. Hanley Webb, with a stranger on either side of him, was motioning Jaydee to pull up. "This here is Jaydee Mooney, Mrs. Hoots. I want ye to meet the gol-durndest jockey in the country." He winked at Rosa. "He's a feisty fellow, not near so easy to handle as Black Gold."

Jaydee leaned down and held out his hand. "I'm glad to meet you, ma'am," he said with his best manners.

"And this-here young lady on my left," Webb went on, "is Marjorie Heffering. Her and her family come clear from Canady for the Derby. Her Pa owns twenty-five head. Him and Al Hoots was real good friends in the old days."

Now turning to the girl, he said, "Marjorie, meet Jaydee Mooney. Up to now he's allus liked horses better'n girls." He guffawed. "Up to now, mind ye! Ha, ha!"

"Pleased to meet you." Jaydee gave a stiff nod. Self-consciously he bent down and tightened his girth strap another notch.

Marjorie smiled. "Mrs. Hoots has asked me to stand in the centerfield with her during your race. She says she'd feel all boxed-in in the grandstand."

"Fine," said Jaydee. "Near the flagpole'd be the best place to see. That's right by the finish line. 'Fraid I have to go now, Mrs. Hoots; and would you excuse me, miss? I got my road work to do and I got to walk the track before the harrows come and churn things up so I can't see the holes and wet spots."

Up in the jockey quarters he changed quickly into his thick road-work clothes. On his way out of the building, Ben Jones, now a famous trainer, hailed him, took a newspaper clipping out of his billfold. "Thought you'd be interested to see this, Mooney," he said. "Quite a piece about Black Gold. 'Way back in Chickasha, Oklahoma, I saw his mother run her maiden race." The friendly eyes twinkled at the memory. "She gave my Belle Thompson a real run."

"Thanks for the clipping, sir."

"Don't *thank* me, son; it's going to make you fighting mad just like it did me. Sometimes that's a good thing."

Jaydee tucked the clipping into the pocket of his jacket. Plenty of time to read it later. Now he wanted to run, could hardly wait to run; his energy was at the explosion point.

As he ran, there was a great glowing hope inside him. Today was the day for which all of Black Gold's life had been planned. Slowing his swift pace to a dogtrot, he thought of the man Al Hoots, and wished he had known him, wished he could talk with him now. Maybe Mr. Hoots would have something

127

special to say to him, a bit of last-minute advice. Or maybe he'd give him some little good-luck piece—a rabbit's foot, or a shamrock, even.

So strong were his thoughts that he was running again, running unaware of the people in his way—men jumping aside to make room for him, girls turning to stare as he flew past. To him they were no more animate than trees.

He looked at his watch. It was almost eleven. Only a few hours left. At top speed he turned in at the track. The harrows would be at work soon.

He threaded his way through the crowd and down to the starting line. Earnestly he lined himself up in the Number One position, then ran the whole distance of the track, finding the best footing, mapping out in his mind the holes where Black Gold might be thrown off stride, the wet spots where he might slip. Breathless, but with the map fixed sharp and clear, he crossed the finish line. And there, lying in the dirt at his feet, glinting through the dirt, was a thin, race-shined horseshoe.

"My lucky piece!" he shouted. Eagerly he picked it up, and with a joyous swipe dusted it on the seat of his pants. He raised it skyward, almost in salute. "Thank you! Thank you, Al Hoots!" he laughed. *"Now we'll do it."*

Chief Johnson was looking for him in the jockey rooms. "Sweat too long not good," he warned. "I give you time until sun makes smallest shadow."

"Look what I found, Chief!" Jaydee held up the horseshoe. "I'm going to have it chromed for keeps."

"Is good sign." The Chief chuckled sheepishly. "Indians make secret signs for luck, too. Many Osages here last night." With a grin the little man was off, heading for the stables.

Jaydee sat down on a bench in front of his locker. The

room was warm, and he could feel the sweat pouring out of him. As he slipped the horseshoe into his pocket, his fingers found the news clipping about Black Gold. Leaning against the locker, he began to read, slowly:

. . . The fiftieth running of the Kentucky Derby has lost some of the glamour it was expected to have. The most colorful eastern candidates—St. James, Sarazen, Wise Counselor—have all been eliminated through mishaps or failures to train properly. Thus the bulk of attention is centered on the dwarf-like western entry from Oklahoma, Black Gold.

Jaydee slapped his towel against the side of the bench. "For Pete's sake, is this a race between horses, or is it East against West!" He read on, now skimming the lines:

. . . this son of Black Toney and U-see-it, the mare once outlawed from the recognized tracks, constitutes the one-horse stable of Mrs. R. Hoots of Oklahoma. He was considered one of the "joke candidates" earlier in the year because of his small size. Furthermore, winter horses never win Derbies, say the experts.

Anger burned in Jaydee. "One-horse stable! What's wrong with that—if the one horse is Black Gold!" Furious at the whole tone of the article, Jaydee went on to the final insult:

. . . But whatever the result, Kentucky's Golden Derby will be something of an experience. And a victory by the wrong horse is not enough to rob the spectator of the thrill that such a race can give.

Jaydee took that piece of newspaper in his fist, and slowly, fiercely, crumpled it. And slowly, in perfect control, he walked to the waste basket at the end of the room. With a savage toss, he threw the wadded paper into the basket. "So the wrong horse might win, might he!"

22. *Golden Jubilee*

CHURCHILL DOWNS, Saturday, May 17, 1924.
Sunlight and blue shadow! And something in the air that's alive. Not touchable, Jaydee thought, but there all the same. Maybe the air itself alive, breathing at you, whispering hotly in your ear: "This is the day! The day of the Kentucky Derby!"

Look sharp, Jaydee. Fix the picture in your mind. Take quick, separate looks. See the people pouring into the stands for the early races. See them flowing out from the underpass, filling the terraces in the centerfield. Skim the crowd, Jaydee.

Can you see Mrs. Hoots? Maybe she'll watch just your race. Make binoculars of your hands. Oh, there she is, and the girl, too. They found the spot by the flagpole all right. Who are all those black-hatted men with them? I know! They're the Osage tribesmen.

Pull the sunlit scene together, Jaydee. The brown track, the sprinkling carts flinging quick rainbows in their spray, harrows chewing up the dirt with gleaming teeth of steel.

Listen, too, Jaydee! Looking is not enough. Hear the bugles for those other races. Try to live through them, Jaydee. Your time is coming. Hear the excited hum like the swarming of a thousand bees, hear the caller announcing race after race, hear the rataplan of hoofs, and the shouts.

Now stop listening, stop looking. It's time to be doing, Jaydee. Hurry to the jockeys' room. Joke with Pony McAtee, Ivan Parke, Earl Sande, and the others—if you can. You can't? Then put on the rose-colored silks. Remember the Old Stumptown Track, Jaydee? And you perched there on the fence, cheering the colors in? Now go down to the paddock behind the grandstand.

Fifteen minutes left. Fifteen minutes before your bugle.

"Ready, boy?" Old Man Webb speaking.

"Ready."

Weigh in, Jaydee. One hundred fourteen pounds? And the three-and-a-half-pound saddle? And the two-and-a-half-pound lead pad? Now add the lead weights, three pounds on each side—the two-pound slabs in the pockets nearest the withers, next the one-pounders. Watch the hands on the scale, Jaydee. One hundred twenty-six pounds?

One hundred twenty-six.

Ready?

131

Ready.

And Old Man Webb saddling, and Black Gold ready, with green ribbons braided into his mane and tail for the luck of the Irish. Now let the old man give you a leg up, Jaydee.

Listen to the quiet in the paddock, the hushed, whispery quiet. Trainers curving hands around their mouths, giving last-minute orders. Jockeys' heads bent, nodding. Only Hanley Webb giving no advice. Just a half smile: "It's all up to you, Jaydee."

It is four thirty-five by the clock on the scoreboard. There! The bugle! The sweet brassy notes splitting the wind.

Ta—ta—ta; ta,ta,ta,ta; ta,ta,ta,ta; ta,ta,ta,ta-a-a-a!

"Come out on the track!" it calls. "Come out, all you Thoroughbreds! Come out for the Kentucky Derby! The Golden Jubilee!"

The horses quiver with excitement. Down the paddock lane they dance, out between the grandstand and the clubhouse, out toward the track. All nineteen entries eager, yet stepping gingerly, saving their thunder for the big moment. Black Gold, the Number One horse, going upheaded, follows the lead pony.

Now the band strikes up the familiar, haunting melody, "My Old Kentucky Home." And suddenly, as if this were a signal of release for all the pent-up feeling for this moment and this place, eighty thousand voices burst forth:

"The sun shines bright in the old Kentucky home,
 'Tis summer, the darkies are gay;
 The corn-top's ripe and the meadow's in the bloom,
 While the birds make music all the day. . . .
 Weep no more, my lady; oh, weep no more—"

Sing, Jaydee! Glory in your heart. Sing to Black Gold's capering. Sing to the springy rhythm of his legs.

Out of the tail of your eye see the colors, Jaydee, the gay racing jackets bobbing along behind you—Colonel Bradley's green and white, the light blue of Whitney, the purple and yellow for Wheatley Stables; green caps, brown caps, cherry-red caps with gold tassels—on and on in single file behind you.

This is it! This, the moment for which nineteen horses have been bred, trained, keyed. The crowd knows it. Wave on wave the people rise up out of their seats, saluting the horses.

Past the stands, galloping in their warm-up, whetting the eagerness of the fans, the horses parade toward the barrier. The starter is ready, hand on lever, his eye sweeping the entries.

Now the caller's voice blaring out post positions: "Black Gold number one, Transmute two, Klondyke three, King Gorin four, Revenue Agent five, Thorndale six, Altawood seven, Cannon Shot eight, Mad Play nine, Beau Butler ten, Wild Aster eleven, Bracadale twelve, Chilhowee thirteen, Bob Tail fourteen, Diogenes fifteen, Modest sixteen, Mr. Mutt seventeen, Baffling eighteen, and Nautical nineteen."

Ready, ready, ready?

But wait! Diogenes breaks out of line, snaps the webbing, charges down the track. Wait for him to be led back.

Once more the starter is ready, but now Black Gold is jostled out of position. Jaydee feels a jolting body kick to his mount. Wheel around, Jaydee. Save Black Gold from more jarring. Come up to the line again.

At last!

The starter pulls the lever. The web flips into the air. With one voice the crowd roars, "They're off!"

Nineteen bullets of horseflesh burst across the line. Black Gold is third, sixteen jockeys gunning for him, knowing he's the horse to beat. Bracadale, from far on the outside, cuts short across the oncoming field, bumps Black Gold into the rail at the sixteenth pole. Wild Aster, Baffling, Chilhowee join in the interference, blocking him front, back, and on the outside.

Sit tight, Jaydee! Sit tight! Don't let them jump on Black Gold's heels. *Save his heels.* Hold him! You've got the best horse and they know it. Hold him until the first turn. Then weave your way out of the pack.

From third place Black Gold is squeezed back to fourth, to fifth. He's helpless—buried alive by horses on all sides of him, pocketing him, pinching him off.

Jaydee's lungs seem pinched, too, but his quick brain telegraphs, "Hold tight, still! Wait it out!" Pellets of dirt ping through the air, sting his face. Jaydee narrows his eyes to slits, sees through the dirt, sees Black Gold flatten his ears, feels him galvanize for action. The little stallion is ready to drill his way out. "Give me room!" he all but trumpets. "Do something, Jaydee! There's a horse on the inside, a horse on my heels, a horse crowding me on the outside. What are jockeys *for?* Give me room!"

In answer, Jaydee lays the flat of his hand on the hip of the outside horse, firmly pushes that horse away. He has to! He's allowed to! The jockey will not make room for him. But still the pack is too tight. Take him back, Jaydee! Back to seventh place. Ride him wide around the offender, wide on the outside.

Black Gold is finally free, on his own! He hurtles forward . . . gaining, gaining . . . sixth place, fifth place, fourth.

But is he too late? Chilhowee kites out in front of him, crowds him, forces him back to sixth place again.

The half-mile coming up! And once more the whole bunch is closing in tight, tighter, locking him in. Sixth at the half!

Jaydee's mind shouts: "Start the whole thing over? Yes, start over. Take him back again. There's time yet. Swing him wide. Give him his head!"

The track is fast, and now Black Gold makes it lightning fast. Low to the ground, stretching all out, he plunges forward, looks Wild Aster in the eye, passes him, inches up on Transmute, passes him.

Now at the head of the stretch Sande on Bracadale and Johnson on Chilhowee are fighting it out for the lead. Black Gold aims toward them, coming up from behind, pounds his way up on the outside, closing the gap, coming alongside the leaders.

Nothing can stop him!

Nothing?

Suddenly out of nowhere a man appears dead ahead. A man with camera, tripod, and flapping black cloth.

Black Gold props, freezes! He loses stride, falls behind the leaders, a half length, a length, two lengths!

He will lose the race . . . unless . . . unless?

Cluck to him, boy! *Do* something! Desperate now, Jaydee clucks like some mother hen willing her frightened chick forward, clucks with all his heart.

It works! The will to win beats down the fear. Black Gold regains his stride, reaches on for the leaders. In one glorious burst of speed he catches them, races alongside them a split second, then in a slashing drive crosses the line to win! By half a length he wins!

The crowd is pulled to its feet, screaming, roaring. Men are tumbling down from their seats, vaulting the rails, running down the track, bent on touching the winner, touching the jockey. Who but a champion could win such a race? Everything against him from the start. Booted, bumped, boxed in; then near the wire the black cloth scarecrow. Yet he wins!

What a race! What a champion! What a Jubilee!

Two minutes, five and one-fifth seconds—that is all it took. Now it's all over. Lifetimes of effort . . . thousands of miles traveled . . . millions of dollars spent. Work, sweat, grief, joy. Dreams dreamed.

And now it is done.

Horse and jockey can breathe again. They both suck in great lungfuls of air as they come slowly back. Black Gold knows there is no need to hurry any more. His pace has a majestic slowness; he senses the greatness of the moment and is savoring it to the full.

Old Man Webb is limping out on the track to meet them, his ancient topcoat billowing out behind. Jaydee stares, pulls up in midstride. The old man has put on his "respectable" leather collar, but it is dark with sweat, as if he had run the race himself. Jaydee looks down at the exuberant face.

"Well, by gum, the two of ye did it!" the old man grins— a wide, pearly grin.

Even in this moment of triumph, Jaydee cannot help blinking. "Holy mackerel," he gasps, "you're wearing your teeth, too!"

With a nod, half proud, half embarrassed, Webb turns and in great dignity leads Black Gold to the winner's circle out in the centerfield. As Black Gold plants his feet in the turf, the crowd eddies around him, watching with eyes and heart both. Together the old man and Jaydee accept the magnificent horseshoe of roses, the award of the fiftieth anniversary of the Run for the Roses. Gently, they settle the great floral piece about Black Gold's neck.

And now more roses, a great sheaf of them, are held up to Jaydee. One-handed, he takes and holds them awkwardly. "Roses are right for Black Gold," he laughs, "not for me!" His eyes sweep the crowd, searching for Mrs. Hoots. Quickly he dismounts, hands the reins to Webb, and pushes his way to her through the noisy, affectionate mob.

"For you," his words breathless, his eyes shining.

Rosa holds them close one brief moment. With a look to Jaydee that asks for understanding, she turns to the girl at her side. "For you, Marjorie. They are more right for young girls."

Afterward, Jaydee could never remember how he found his way through the surge of people and climbed the steps to the judges' stand. He did remember the famous Matt Winn standing beside the Governor. But he could never recall more than one sentence in all of the Governor's speech:

"We congratulate a little stallion who raced big."

Words flowed over him, around him, through him. Then Colonel Winn stepped forward, smiling, and placed the grand gleaming golden cup in the calm hands of Rosa Hoots. He turned next to Old Man Webb and gave a gold stop watch into his calloused hands. Then it was Jaydee's turn. With shy pride his hot sweaty hands grasped the Golden Jubilee spurs. His own! His, to put with the lucky horseshoe.

The people went wild. The air crackled with their applause and cheering. Over and over Colonel Winn and the Governor pleaded for silence. At last, into the trough between waves of clamor, came the slow, deep voice of Rosa Hoots over the loudspeaker. "My husband," she said, "he dreamed that U-see-it's

140

colt would win this race and make right the evil that came to her. Black Gold and Mooney, they both did their best. I owe it to them," she finished.

The microphone went next to Hanley Webb. He cleared his throat nervously, but no sound came. Desperately he thrust the mouthpiece at Jaydee.

The boy wanted the chance. "Black Gold ran his own race!" he nearly shouted. "Any other horse would've lost. *The right horse won.*"

23. The Magic Shoe

LIKE A brush fire in the wind Black Gold's popularity spread. The very newspapers that had made little of him now headlined: NATION'S FAVORITE WINS. WEST TRIUMPHS OVER EAST.

Black Gold was a hero! Even though it was only the middle of May, men called him the horse of the year. Everything he did made news. If he kicked his water bucket to smithereens, some reporter was on hand to take a picture. If he had a sniffle, it caused wide concern.

People everywhere gathered him into their hearts. Oklahomans affectionately called him "the pride of the Osages." Kentucky referred to him as *"their* Black Toney's son." Louisiana adopted him not only because he ran his first race there, but was not his jockey born and bred in New Orleans? The rest of the nation just plain loved him for his spirit.

"Where will he race next?" was the question on everyone's tongue. Thick as raindrops the invitations came—by telephone, by telegram, by mail. "Black Gold is good for the sport of racing," the messages said. "We hereby invite you to enter him in the Ohio State Derby . . . the Chicago Derby . . . the Tri-State Fair at Ashland, Kentucky . . . the autumn meeting of the Kentucky Jockey Club."

Old Man Webb was beside himself with joy. He could not say No. He believed that Black Gold was invincible, like some legendary horse of old, and he wanted to prove it. Sure! Had he not been racing as a two-year-old when most colts are just "prepping up?" Now he must go on adding more stars to his crown. It was his destiny!

So . . . less than a week after the Kentucky Derby, Black Gold was winning the Ohio State Derby. By ten lengths! "What did I tell ye?" the old man beamed. "There's no stopping him!"

Only a few wise men wondered if the willing horse should be raced less and rested more.

And then, on June 23 at Latonia, Black Gold finished last in a field of seven horses, many of whom he had vanquished in the Kentucky Derby. It was the first loss for the team of Black Gold and Jaydee Mooney. Was it the soreness in his foot showing up again—the same trouble he'd had the week before the Derby? Or was it the sticky condition of the track?

"'Twas the gumbo track, a-course," Old Man Webb insisted.

But five days later over a fast track Black Gold and Jaydee could not quite catch the leaders. They had to take third place. "Your timing is off!" Hanley Webb accused Jaydee. "You're coddling him."

"I have to! It's that foot again, sir. Maybe we really oughta give him a rest."

"Don't be ridic'lous! We'll give him more work! That's what fixed him afore the Derby; and 'twill again."

It was Jaydee who discovered what was wrong with Black Gold. After a third race lost, he took the shoe pullers, pried off the thin racing shoe, and started to explore. At first everything seemed quite all right. The wedge-shaped frog in the center of the hoof was nice and cushiony, as it should be. Then he cleaned out the foot carefully and began studying the inside wall.

It's sound, he thought, and perfectly bell-shaped. Then he noticed what seemed to be one of the colt's own black hairs embedded in the hoof wall. But when he tried to pick it out, he found it was not a hair at all. A very fine crack went all the way up inside the hoof.

Could this be a quarter crack? A knife-edge of fear twisted into the core of Jaydee. Still holding Black Gold's hoof between his knees, he thought hard. Other horses have had quarter cracks, but what was the cure? Was there a cure? There had to be!

Gently he put the hoof down and peered into the next stall, looking for Hanley Webb. Chief Johnson sat there alone, sewing tapes on one of Black Gold's blankets. He spoke without turning his head.

"Webb gone to town," he said. "He buy groceries. And carrots for all."

Jaydee felt an overpowering need to do something now. This very minute. He ran over toward the blacksmith tent, banty chicks scuttering out of the way, goats almost tripping him.

144

"Smith!" he yelled. "Mr. Buschor!" he called the man's name.

The smith, a burly man with grizzled whiskers, was rolling down his sleeves, ready to stop work for the day. "What's all the ruckus?" he asked, hanging up his tongs.

"Come quick!" Jaydee pleaded.

"Emergency?"

145

"Oh, yes, sir! I just found a crack in Black Gold's foot. Couldn't that be what's making him go lame?"

No reply came, but together they hurried back to the stable. "Which foot?" asked Buschor as they reached Black Gold's stall.

"Left front, sir. There must be something we can do . . . isn't there?"

But the smith was concentrating, running his horny fingers along the crack and then up to the knee.

"I've had cases like this before," he said at last.

"And what'd you do?"

"I built a bar plate across the heel of the shoe," he answered matter-of-factly.

Jaydee saw the shoe in his mind. "It'll keep the crack from getting wider, won't it?"

"It will. And it'll ease all that soreness in his foot. But," he lifted a warning finger, "'twon't be no permanent cure. It's only a makeshift."

Old Man Webb came striding along just then, his arms loaded with groceries. He stormed into Black Gold's stall. "What's going on here?" he puffed.

"I just chanced to be going by," the smith said, "and I was kinda curious about what was making Black Gold go gimpy."

"Truth is, *I* asked him to come in," Jaydee confessed.

The old man snorted. "Now that you two've been conniving, what did you find?"

"Nothin' but what a bar shoe'll fix. Temporary, that is."

"Contraptions!" Webb barked, and his mouth drew down at the corners. "They rankle me. That's why I never go to the trottin' tracks with their horses all crutched up with hobbles and poles and boots and breast collars." He looked the smith in the eye. "When I want ye, *I'll* do the calling. Don't pay no mind to Jaydee; he's a worrier."

Five days later, after another race lost, Old Man Webb himself sent for the blacksmith. "All right," he agreed reluctantly. "Go ahead. We'll try that shoe."

Some said the shoe was magic. But the smith knew better. He knew it took more than a shoe to win the Chicago Derby. Even the trainers of the other entries admitted that any other horse with any other jockey would have given up. Going into the back stretch, Black Gold was a full forty lengths behind the leader. Yet he won!

Newspapers from coast to coast carried the story. The *New York Times* gave it almost a column. "We salute a game fighter," they said, "a horse who can run all day with his head in the air. The farther he goes, the greater his speed."

"See?" Old Man Webb shook his fist happily just two inches under Jaydee's nose. "There's stamina for you! That horse is made o' iron! He'll race forever!"

24. *Critical Decision*

B UT THE smith was more of a prophet than Hanley Webb.
The bar shoe gave only temporary relief, and the quarter
crack widened. Yet in spite of his tortured foot, Black Gold kept
on racing, and by sheer will power won his races. Now, people
somehow began to identify themselves with him. If he could go
on winning over such a handicap, they too could go on living
with their own lameness, deafness, whatever their burden.

But near the close of the racing season that year, Jaydee
could stand Black Gold's suffering no longer. On his way home
late one evening he noticed a light in the blacksmith's tent and
went inside.

"Mr. Buschor?"

The man turned in surprise. "Oh, it's you," he said, his face sobering to match Jaydee's. "What is it, Mooney?"

"It's about Black Gold. The bar plate on his shoe doesn't help any more."

"Whyn't you tell me something I ain't already seen with my own eyes?" the smith asked brusquely. Then he added in a kinder tone, "Cheer up, fella. Nothin's ever so bad but what it could be worsened or bettered. Set down on that keg over there and just let me finish up this shoe for King's Ransom. We can chin while I work."

Marking time, Jaydee picked up a sliver of hoof trimming and put it in his pocket. "Nothing Buster prizes more," he said, "than a fresh piece of hoof to chew on and to play with. Black Gold's certainly no playmate any more."

"'Tain't no wonder!" the smith sputtered. He took off his apron and hung it on a nail. "Now," he said, looking very directly at Jaydee, "what Black Gold needs is an operation."

"Operation!" The quick sound of fear showed in Jaydee's voice.

"Hold on, boy. 'Tain't that serious. But mind ye, there's got to be two steps to it."

"What are they, sir?"

"First ye rest him. About a month or so, I'd say. Just turn him out on some good springy turf and let him go barefoot."

"And then?"

"Why, the operation, a-course." The smith answered cheerfully, trying to give the boy courage. "It's simple as A B C to a good vet. He just takes his knife, a real sharp 'un, and he cuts a groove along each side of the crack."

"Yes?"

"And then he takes a pair o' nippers and pulls out the piece of hoof between the two grooves."

Jaydee flinched.

"Oh, stop yer worritin'. 'Tain't so dreadful as all that. Nearest I can tell ye, it's like peeling an onion. Or maybe it's more like pulling a hangnail."

"Then what happens?"

"Why, the new wall of the hoof grows right down so smooth you wouldn't know there'd ever been a crack. He'll race as good as ever." He paused. "Only one thing serious about this whole job."

"What's that?" Jaydee asked quickly.

"If it ain't done."

Instead of going home, Jaydee turned back toward the stable. He couldn't go home. This was so important he had to tell Webb first. He must stop him from planning any more races.

Black Gold and Buster, Old Man Webb and the Chief, were all bedded down for the night when Jaydee poked his head in the door.

"You awake?" he whispered.

The old man snorted. " 'Course I'm awake; that's how I sleep." A troubled sigh came from the bunk bed. "I been layin' here, wondering if Buschor could trim Black Gold's foot and reset the bar plate so's he could finish out the season."

"No." Jaydee's voice was quiet, firm, resolute. "Black Gold's got to rest and then the quarter crack has got to be cut out."

"So? You been consultin' with Buschor again?"

"I didn't want to, sir, but I'm going away. Far away."

"You're *what?*" The old man sat bolt upright.

Jaydee was glad for the darkness. The words surprised even himself. They had suddenly spilled out. If Black Gold had to

150

go on racing, he could no longer be a party to it, and if Black Gold had his operation, there would be no racing for months. Then he would have to go to the owners who had asked him to race before, and somehow he couldn't bring himself to do this.

"Look-a-here, Jaydee. I been boss and father both to ye. Ain't you making a muckle of a mickle? You sure about going away?"

"I never *was* so sure, Mister Webb. If ever I'm to ride him again, Black Gold has to have that quarter crack fixed."

The Indian Chief turned and grunted in his sleep.

"But where? Where are you going?" Webb asked.

"I don't have the least idea. Only I just got to get out of here. Far as I can go. Maybe California or Canada." Suddenly he thought of the girl who had stood in the centerfield with Mrs. Hoots during the Derby. Her father had twenty-five head of horses and was an old friend of Mr. Hoots. "Yes, I might even go clean out of the country—to Canada," Jaydee said. "Maybe that Mr. Hefferman could put me in touch with folks who need a jockey or a trainer."

"Heffering," the old man corrected testily. "Not Hefferman."

Black Gold sneezed just then, and the old man's resistance turned to ashes. What he saw now in the darkness was the truth. His eyes had known it a long time, but his mind had said No to all the signs—to the growing harshness of the coat, the puny appetite, the ribs beginning to show, the listless look.

"Jaydee," he said into the night, "I been a cranky, stubborn-headed old fool. The why of it ain't no matter to a young man like you. You've a Ma to love you and a Grandma, and some day a girl, but . . ."

Jaydee caught the hurt in the old man's voice. "But what?" he asked gently.

151

"Well . . . it's just . . . I got no one. No family at all. No kinfolk anywheres that I know of. Before Black Gold began racin' to fame, my world was flat as a prairie. Then all of a sudden I seemed to be livin' for the first time. For oncet I seemed to be kinda important."

He paused and the sigh that escaped him sounded big and lonely. Buster leaped through the partition, jumped up on his cot, and lay close, his muzzle fitting snugly in the old man's shoulder.

"I guess," Webb went on, "I figgered my world'd go all dead and empty again if Black Gold stopped racing."

Jaydee tried to comfort him. "It'll only be part of a season." But the man interrupted.

"I been a fool, boy," he repeated in misery. "Sacrificin' him for the likes of me." He got up, shuffling across the stall in his nightshirt. "The shock of all you said must've jounced the truth into me." He put his hand on Jaydee's shoulder and shook it gently. "All right! I'll take him to the Blue Grass country. I'll rest him. Then he can have his operation, and come spring, the three of us'll start off again with nothing but wins. Eh, boy?"

25. *Without a Backward Glance*

NEXT MORNING Jaydee came to Black Gold's stall dressed in his good suit. He had with him a fistful of redtop clover which he had cut with his pocketknife along the roadside.

"I'm going far away," he whispered as he offered a tuft of clover on the flat of his hand. "But I'll be back soon—in the spring, that is. Meantime I got to work to earn my keep, and you can eat and play and get sleek again, and have your operation. Then we'll be thundering down the homestretch again, with the wind singin' in our ears."

Suddenly he could talk no more. He had to go. Quietly he

slid under the door straps, picked up his bag and grasped Webb's gnarled old hand. With a look and a nod for the Chief, he turned and ran down the shed row, Buster at his heels. When Buster stopped at the end of the row and sat down on his stub of a tail, Jaydee knew the good-by's had been said.

He knew, too, that his big dream had been fulfilled, but already a new one was taking its place. Black Gold would have the greatest comeback in the history of the turf.

Up in Canada the fall wore itself out. Sugar maples turned to gold in the dark October woods, then showered their leaves for the wind to scatter.

As winning jockey of the Kentucky Derby, Jaydee was much sought after, particularly in training matters now. Owners liked the way he handled horses. The very young ones he sometimes schooled without even mounting them. He drove them around the ring, his voice spurring or coaxing as the need arose.

He was riding some good horses, too. He won the King's Plate at Woodbine in Toronto. But after the race, when he gave the shining trophy to Marjorie Heffering, she read his mind. "Even the good horses seem big and bumbling alongside Black Gold, don't they?"

Winter came on, and the work never let up. Jaydee was glad of it, glad with a kind of fierce gladness. But all the while he kept wondering about Black Gold. What of the operation? Was it painful? When had it been? Was it successful? As the days went their slow way, he grew more and more impatient. In February he wrote a card to Old Man Webb, but got no answer. He had really expected none.

By April he could control his impatience no longer. The time clock in his mind said, "You *must* go. Now." And he went.

It was already spring in Kentucky—dogwood and redbud blooming on the mountainsides, cardinals staking out their claims in song, bluegrass rippling in the wind. But as the train pulled into Lexington, Jaydee was hardly aware of the signs of spring. Like an eager colt at the barrier, he was first out of the train. In the station washroom he quickly changed from his suit to the old work clothes.

A white-haired gentleman looked on in amusement, his nose twitching like a rabbit's. "You've something to do with horses," he laughed. "Mind if I ask why you're changing here?"

"I'm going to see Black Gold. I want to help him remember me," Jaydee grinned.

"Black Gold!" the man's face showed recognition and astonishment. "Why, he's on my neighbor's place. I live up the road only a little piece yonder. I'll give you a lift, if you like."

They drove between green pastures criss-crossed with white fences, saw mares and foals grazing in the sun. To Jaydee the whole countryside looked so green and rain-washed that he grew doubly impatient to see what the springy turf had done for his horse.

He was suddenly alive, every fiber of him vibrating with strong feelings. Almost before the car stopped, he was out of it, barely thanking the driver. He had a need to run, to find Black Gold at once, to see, to see! He ran up the lane, whipping past the stable office, and out of breath reached at last a small paddock. There a lone black horse stood grazing. Jaydee stopped dead still. Was it, or was it not, Black Gold? Perhaps it was some younger stallion, some two-year-old who had never known the hard work of the track, who had never felt the lead weights in his saddle. Perhaps it was another of Black Toney's colts.

Look further, Jaydee. There's a bigger paddock up there

155

on the knoll. No, wait! The muscled, shining stallion is coming your way. Wait! See the wind lifting his forelock? The white mark is there.

"Hey, young feller, want to gallop him?" came a rough, familiar voice.

Jaydee's laughter rang out over the hills. "Do I!" he shouted.

And now the old man and Jaydee embracing like father and son, and Black Gold nudging them with his muzzle.

On went the bridle, the eager horse reaching to take the bit. On went the saddle. Up went Jaydee as if he were twelve, not twenty. Away at a brisk walk went Black Gold out onto the exercise ring.

Once around at a walk. Once again. Then with bated breath Jaydee signaled him to go. Black Gold did his best for the boy he understood so well, but after a short gallop he pulled up dead lame.

Old Man Webb was alongside Jaydee in a moment. "Shoulda told you . . . maybe right off . . . You see . . . uh . . . we didn't cut out the quarter crack. He didn't have that operation. I thought . . ."

A deep and terrible anger flared up in Jaydee. "You thought what?" he almost screamed.

The old man lowered his head. "I figgered he'd get better without it, and I didn't want to worry Mrs. Hoots. . . . But don't he look good?"

Jaydee never answered. He bent forward in the saddle, and pressing the side of his face hard against Black Gold's neck, he let the hot tears come.

When his sobs finally quieted, he dismounted and grimly handed the reins to Hanley Webb. Then he strode back to the paddock, numbly picked up his grip, and without a backward glance trudged downward along the path up which he had raced so short a time ago.

The old man watched, disconsolate, until the forlorn figure was nothing but a speck far down the road. He knew he would never see the boy again.

26. *Green Pastures*

FOR SOME time Black Gold lived on in the same paddock where Jaydee had found him. He seemed reasonably content. Old Man Webb continued to let him go barefoot, and how good it felt to be rid of those shoes! With each step his feet were cooled and moistened by the living green carpet.

And he liked the freedom of being out of doors where he could see the comings and goings of horses and men, and could feel the warmth of the sun getting through to his bones. The smells, too, he liked—from the early pear blossoms of spring to the aromatic smell of mint and boxwood in the hot summer sun, to the fall sweetness of clover-rich hay.

A few mares were brought to him to be bred, but he sired only one foal. When a bolt of lightning struck and killed it before it was a month old, Hanley Webb took the tragedy as an omen. Black Gold should have no more colts.

So he spent his days alone, in quiet routine. Eat, sleep. Sleep, eat. Week in, week out. Days without end.

But one blowy autumn afternoon Black Gold's tranquil world exploded. A remembered sound was borne to him on the wind. It was the thin clear treble of the bugle. *Ta—ta—ta; ta, ta, ta, ta!* The signal he knew! A race was about to begin!

He could see across the meadows the line of horses coming out on the private track over at Idle Hour Farm. *He* should be there! The bugle was calling *him!* How could he *get* there? Trembling violently, he threw back his head and sent out a great aching cry that held all of longing and loneliness. Now, faintly on the wind he heard the shout, "They're off!"

The sound pulled a trigger in his mind. He bolted to the fence rail, began galloping wildly around his paddock. The blood pounded hotly through him. He was leaving the other horses behind. Far behind! He was living again—wind singing past him, no one blocking him, no one holding him back. For sheer joy he extended himself, gave all the speed he had in him. All by himself he won the race! Going away he won it!

Limping a little, he walked proudly to the corner of the paddock nearest Idle Hour Farm. The distant applause must

be for him. The sound made him feel tingly and warm. He tossed his head skyward and this time the whinny that rang across the countryside was one of ecstasy.

Now Black Gold knew what to do with his solitary days. Each afternoon he put on a race of his own until, in time, he had worn an oval track in the turf.

"Will you look at that, now!" Old Man Webb exclaimed to the flocks of children who came daily to watch Black Gold run. "He's tramped out his own track. He's a racing horse, he is. Ain't nothing going to stop him!"

But, in contrast to Black Gold's new-found happiness, Hanley Webb began to droop. As the months wore on, he became a pitiable creature. His whole figure seemed to wilt. The eyes, usually so bright and alert, had a look of yearning for remembered places and doings. It was the Christmas season that broke his spirit, the Christmas of 1926. All at once these years of loneliness became a load too heavy to bear. Were he and Black Gold forever retired? Was an imaginary track, imaginary racing, imaginary living the best they could do?

"I've no one to sew so much as a button for me, or to care whether I live or die," he told Colonel Bradley one day. "And Black Gold has nary a foal to carry his torch neither. Mebbe," he said with a flicker of hope, "mebbe him and me should go into the racing business again, by'n by."

A look of shock, almost horror, crossed the Colonel's face. "Have you forgotten his quarter crack?"

Old Man Webb took off his hat and reamed the inside of it. "No, I ain't forgot," he said slowly, thoughtfully. "But he allus did pull up lame, Colonel. Then ye'd cool him out, and he'd go sound as a dollar again."

The Colonel drew in a breath. "Well, you're his trainer, Webb." And he turned away abruptly, pulling hard at his cigar.

On a crisp December day two weeks later, Old Man Webb. a satchel in one hand and a halter rope in the other, was leading Black Gold down the old Frankfort Pike to the railroad station. As he walked, he tried not to see the families decorating their Christmas trees with lights and tinsel. Alone, with no grooms in attendance, he loaded Black Gold into a boxcar bound for New Orleans.

161

" 'Twill be warmer down there," he said to himself, watching his breath make a cloud of vapor. He huddled down into a corner of the car, pulled his worn topcoat about him, and tried to fasten the lone button dangling by a thread.

27. A Penny Postcard

I T WAS warmer in New Orleans. Poinsettias were in bloom. Vines were green and clambering everywhere. The old man sighed in satisfaction. It was so good to be back in Louisiana, and good to be training again.

Almost upon his arrival he found a freckle-spattered boy to exercise Black Gold. "Don't try to be another Jaydee," he said brusquely, " 'cause you can't do it. But here's what I got in mind. I want Black Gold to win the big New Orleans Handicap in February. But afore then, we got to get a new bar shoe made and put him in some little test races. So you start tuning him up. Go two or three miles every day. But slow, mind ye; *slow*."

Once more the old routine began, like the good, monotonous hand-turning of a grindstone. But the speed in Black Gold never sharpened enough to satisfy the old man's expectations. Nor did the test races do much to build up his confidence. More and more often the thought recurred, how hamstrung a trainer and a champion are without the right boy in the saddle! Separately we're nothing, he thought to himself, but together we're lightning.

"Together we're harnessed lightning!" he said one night as he sat down discouraged at the battered old table in his stall. Frowning, he almost unwillingly pulled toward him a box of odds and ends. He rummaged among the old programs and blanket pins and pieces of string until he found a penny postcard, dog-eared but still usable. He didn't write immediately. It took courage and humbleness. At last his fingers took up a stub of a pencil and slowly, laboriously the words formed:

Dear Jaydee:
    We are in your home town. Black Gold doing fair—but we could use you, son. Any chance of your visiting your folks soon? Salome Purse comes up 1/18/27. It's like the Derby Trial. If he wins that, he can sure win the New Orleans Handicap 2/4/27. Try to come.

Yrs,

H. Webb

He added a "please," erased it, and was glad when it showed through anyway.

In his quarters on the Heffering ranch, Jaydee found the postcard in his mail on the dresser. He took it wonderingly to the window, and in the gray winter light his eyes followed

the penciled lines. As he read the cramped handwriting, he could see the old man in his threadbare coat, his eyes pleading. And he could see Black Gold—small, brave, and willing to try again. Holding himself in check as tightly as his fingers held the card, he went bare-headed across the snow toward the house. He wanted to share this with someone before he wrote the answer. He knocked, and was glad when Marjorie herself opened the door. Without a word he handed her the card. They went inside, and when she had read, she looked up searchingly.

"What are you going to do, Jaydee?"

His eyes were set far off. He was thinking that all he'd be able to do for Black Gold would not be enough. He could sit bird-light on the little horse's neck. He could cluck to him with heart and soul. He could threaten with the whip. But two things he knew—it would not be enough and it would not be fair.

"What are you going to say?" Marjorie asked.

"A single word'll do it."

" 'Sorry'?"

"Yes, 'Sorry'," Jaydee nodded, feeling such misery that his heart was near to bursting.

28. The Winner Loses

AND SO with Jaydee a thousand miles away, Black Gold was entered in the Salome Purse.

When the day came, the people streaming into the stands were talking mostly of Black Gold; they wanted him to win. Their affection amounted to tenderness. As the field of nine horses answered the bugle, the tumult and the cheering were all for the little stallion trying to make his comeback.

It was a day of days. Brilliant sunshine. Track fast. Entries eager.

The voice over the loud-speaker was filling in time: "Anything can happen on today's track—records may be broken, new heroes made. *Any*thing!" And now the trumpeted words: "The horses are at the post. Nine entries jockeying for position.

Black Gold the Number One horse with young Dave Emery up." The words quickened. "Black Gold's the oldest entry, but he carries more weight than any of the others—up to fifteen pounds more!"

Old Man Webb stands tense and silent at the rail. Old Man Webb thinking: "Black Gold has the Number One position. Just like in the Derby." Then in irritation: "He's ready. Why don't they take off?"

Minutes of precious energy wasted. The four-year-olds rambunctious; the veteran campaigners quiet. One minute. Two minutes. Three. Then a sudden swing into line and "They're off!" the caller yells, and the crowd with him.

Nine horses leaping forward, but binoculars everywhere are focused on the shiny black with the rose-colored silks. He breaks away in the lead, holds it a second, then lets the sprinters race by him.

Webb clenches his fist, his mind following the pattern. "Yep, yep! Ye're racin' true to form, savin' yerself for the stretch!"

With one voice the stands are urging, begging, "Come on, Black Gold! Come on, Black Gold."

"At the quarter pole," the battery of speakers booms above the roar, "it's Dearborn in the lead, Colonel Board second, Polygamia third, Black Gold number four."

Webb's hat is off now, his head shiny with perspiration. His voice and twenty thousand others pleading, "You can do it, Black Gold! You can do it!"

And the caller's powerful voice again: "At the half it's Colonel Board in the lead, Dearborn second, Polygamia third, Black Gold holding on to fourth."

"Go after Polygamia!" Hanley Webb spits out the name. "Polygamia with only a hundred pounds!" His eyes are fixed

167

on the rose-colored jacket, seeing it as a bright fuse burning up the track.

"At the three-quarters," the loud-speaker blares, "it's Colonel Board in the lead, Polygamia in second place, Black Gold third, and gaining."

Third place at the three-quarters! Now at the head of the stretch he is ready for the rush. The very atmosphere quivers with excitement. The stands are on their feet. Webb is beside himself, clucking in anguish, "You can do it! You *got* to!"

Then suddenly the joyousness in the air is torn apart. Thundering down the home stretch, Black Gold bobbles.

"Oh, dear God!" the cry wrenches from the old man as he sees his horse stumble, lose stride, nearly fall, the other horses veering sharp to avoid him. Desperately his jockey tries to stop him, to pull him up, but Black Gold drives on.

For an instant a terrible quiet locks twenty thousand hearts and minds together. Then the question rockets: "What in God's world has happened?"

"Stop him!" the voices scream. "Someone stop him!" But the game horse will not be held in until he crosses the line.

"Black Gold's leg—" the horror-stricken caller shouts to the crowd. "Black Gold's leg," he repeats, "snapped above the ankle. His bandage was all that held it together. But he finished his race—on three legs and a heart he finished it."

Men and women, stunned to silence, watch grooms and veterinarians and a limping old man rush out on the track and try to help Black Gold into the waiting wagon. Even now he resents all the fuss made over him. He tosses his head impatiently, seeming to cry out, "Don't hold me so tight; if that's what you want of me, I can get into the wagon by myself."

His fans are still calling his name, as the tail gate of the wagon is pulled up, as the wagon itself slowly disappears behind the barns.

The voice of the caller goes strangely hoarse. "Ladies and gentlemen," it announces, "Polygamia won the race, but her owner, Mr. Rice, calls it a hollow victory. He says 'the loser really won.' Black Gold, the great-hearted little stallion, insisted on finishing his race. He has just been put to sleep—mercifully, without pain. He has joined the immortals."

The next morning, in the centerfield of the Fair Grounds, Black Gold was buried. There was no sermon and no singing; just a cluster of people with love in their hearts, groping for the right words to say. They were trying to comfort a defeated old man.

"Listen, Webb, he's out of his pain," one said. "To have him other than sound wouldn't be right. You know that."

A woman holding a cross in one hand and a poinsettia in the other said, "Perhaps animals don't have souls, but maybe Black Gold was an exception. And just maybe the Psalms were written for him as well as for the likes of us. 'The Lord ruleth me,' " she quoted as she laid the red flower on his grave, " 'and I shall want nothing. He hath set me in a place of pasture. He hath brought me up on the water of refreshment.' "

Then out of the little cluster of people came trainer Ben Jones. Dear Ben Jones who had known Al Hoots, who had watched U-see-it run her first race, who had known about the dream for her colt. He put his arm about Hanley Webb's shoulders. "The lady's right," he said, his voice husky with kindness. "And what's more, Hanley, I reckon Al Hoots was sittin' up there on a cloud, all ready to welcome Black Gold."

Hanley Webb's smile was half tears.

'Black Gold--Gamest of the Game'

BLACK GOLD'S TRAINER

HANLEY WEBB
RELATES STORY
OF COLT'S LIFE

I TRAINED HIM O
IN NEW YORK

BLACK GOLD M
RECORD N 1924

COLT NOUGH
OKLA FOR
BURD

29. *In Good Faith*

THE HANDWRITING on the newspaper wrapper was
Grandma Mooney's. Jaydee, sitting on the edge of his
bunk, knew already what the paper would contain. And *I
know why she sent it*, he thought. He had half a mind to lay
it aside. No matter what the story said, it couldn't change
things. Nothing would ever be the same. The familiar misery
and bitterness welled up in him again. But in a moment he took

171

a resolute breath; his hands tore off the wrapper and unrolled the *New Orleans Tribune.*

He skimmed the front page. Nothing there. Maybe, he thought, maybe last week's tragedy never happened. Maybe it was only a nightmare. But suddenly the picture on page two leaped up at him. It was Black Gold and he, Jaydee, in the saddle. At New Orleans? At Latonia? At Churchill Downs? Places and times washed together. Then all at once he was back in Black Gold's stall, feeling the quarter crack and hearing the smith's portentous words . . .

"Stop it!" he told himself. "And read! Maybe you'll find a crumb of comfort."

The heading was a long bold streamer:

TRAINER BLAMES SELF FOR BLACK GOLD'S DEATH

And there beneath the horse's picture was a small one of Hanley Webb, bowed low in grief. His old sweat-stained slouch hat was pulled down over a face grim with sorrow.

"I am responsible for his death [the story began]. I never paid any attention to Black Gold's lameness; he always seemed to work out of it. As God is my witness, I ran him in good faith."

A feeling of compassion rose in Jaydee. Now he wished he had been there beside the old man when Black Gold was buried. Anxiously his eyes sought the paper again.

Black Gold's place of burial, [the article went on] is in the centerfield of Fair Grounds Park. It seems somehow right. He was laid to rest where he ran his first race and his last, buried with his head toward the west, toward Oklahoma and Skiatook, the original home of his mother, U-see-it.

The grave is a beautiful spot, with flowering shrubs and poinsettias growing around it. It is only a few yards from the grave of the famous Pan Zaretta, Queen of Texas. She was the only mare that outran U-see-it, and now, with a nice twist of fate, Black Gold has bettered her record.

Jaydee could not help smiling at that. Suddenly his anger at Webb melted completely. He went on to the final paragraph.

The fact that Black Gold died is not as important as the way he died. The caller who made the tragic announcement to the awe-struck crowd, said it best. "He finished his race. On three legs and a heart, he finished it!"

His was the victory of a Thoroughbred.

Jaydee re-folded the newspaper and stood up. He went across the room to his dresser and opened the top drawer. In it he laid the paper, tucking it carefully beneath the chromed horseshoe and the golden spurs. Then slowly he closed the drawer.

He was satisfied.

Now, each year at Fair Grounds Park in New Orleans, a race called the Black Gold Stakes is held in honor of the courageous little stallion. And each year the winning jockey places his wreath of flowers on Black Gold's grave.

Children and grownups gave their pennies and their dollars to build a very special monument. Instead of dry words chiseled into stone there is a smooth curving saddle, so real that it seems to be waiting for Jaydee.

Sometimes Jaydee does come to see the race, and then the winning jockey presents the flowers to him. As he walks slowly, alone, into the centerfield, the stands rise up row on row, and in the hushed silence Jaydee gently decorates the grave of one he loved.

For their help the author is grateful to

BEN JONES, Calumet Farm, Lexington, Kentucky

H. A. (JIMMY) JONES, Calumet Farm, Lexington, Kentucky

OLIN GENTRY, Darby Dan Farm, Lexington, Kentucky

HORACE WADE, Director, Gulf Stream Park, Florida

LEO O'DONNELL, Steward on the Eastern Circuit

AVERY E. BROWN and J. S. PERLMAN, Triangle Publications, Inc., New York and Chicago

J. A. ESTES, Editor of *The Blood Horse,* Lexington, Kentucky

BLANCHE GARRISON, Bartlesville, Oklahoma, niece of Rosa Hoots

F. L. DALE, Skiatook, Oklahoma, friend of the Hoots family

WILLIAM HOGE, Indian historian and columnist for the *Tulsa World*

B. YOREL, Indian weaver, Tulsa, Oklahoma

JAMES E. GOURLEY, Head Librarian, Tulsa Public Library

FLORENCE L. BRALY, Reference Librarian, Tulsa Public Library

ALLIE BESS MARTIN, Head of Extension and Children's Work, Tulsa Public Library

KIM GEORGE, Consultant in Children's Reading, Tulsa Public Library

ROBERTA B. SUTTON, Reference Librarian, Chicago Public Library

IDA G. WILSON, Head Librarian, Gail Borden Public Library, Elgin, Illinois

MILDRED G. LATHROP, Reference Librarian, Gail Borden Public Library, Elgin, Illinois

EUGENIA WHELAN, Head Librarian, Hollywood Public Library, Hollywood, Florida

PEGGY RYDER, Hollywood Public Library, Hollywood, Florida

and especially to

the Mooneys—Marjorie, Jaydee and Paul